D1343841

Dear Reader,

With this book we begin another MIGHTY QUINNS trilogy. Ten years ago, the first Quinn book hit the shelves and to be honest, I never thought I'd still be writing them after all this time. But obviously, there's something about a sexy Irish hero that people find irresistible. I'll admit, I've got a bit of a weakness for them.

I guess you do, too!

I've set Mighty Quinn stories in Boston, New York and even in Australia. But, fittingly, I think, I've put the books that mark a decade of hot Quinn heroes back on the Emerald Isle again.

Although I have only a few drops of Irish blood running through me, there's something about that beautiful country that I find really compelling. It's my hope that you'll feel the same sense of wonder I did, in the pages of this book.

Once you've been charmed by Riley, watch for his equally irresistible brothers, Danny and Kellan, to show up in the Blaze lineup in November and December 2012.

Happy reading,

Kate Hoffmann

THE
MIGHTY QUINNS:
RILEY

BY
KATE HOFFMANN

MILLS &
BOON

First published in Great Britain 2012
by Mills & Boon, an imprint of Harlequin (UK) Limited,
Eton House, 18-24 Paradise Road, Richmond, Surrey TW9 1SR

© Peggy A. Hoffmann 2011

ISBN: 978 0 263 89742 5

30-1012

Harlequin's policy is to use papers that are natural, renewable and recyclable products and made from wood grown in sustainable forests. The logging and manufacturing processes conform to the legal environmental regulations of the country of origin.

Printed and bound in Spain
by Blackprint CPI, Barcelona

Kate Hoffmann began writing for Mills & Boon® in 1993. Since then she's published sixty-five books, primarily in the Blaze® lines. When she isn't writing, she enjoys music, theater and musical theater. She is active working with high school students in the performing arts. She lives in southeastern Wisconsin with her cat, Chloe.

To Birgit Davis-Todd, who gave me the idea for the Mighty Quinns over ten years ago. Thank you!

Prologue

THE LIGHTS IN THE SMALL bedroom had been put out a half hour before, but the three brothers were too occupied with the raging storm outside than with falling asleep. Riley Quinn sat at the window, watching as the rain slashed against the glass. The rosebushes in the garden were bent so low by the wind coming off the sea that they touched the ground.

"Jaysus, it's bucketing out there," Riley said. "Noah and his ark will be floating by any second now."

"Do you think this is like the storm that made Ma fall in love with Da?" Danny asked.

Daniel, the youngest of the three Quinn brothers, sat in the center of his bed, the covers pulled up to his chin. The eight-year-old had an imagination that never seemed to stop. He could see dragons and sea serpents wherever he looked and though he was a bit of a baby, Riley was beginning to like him more as he got older. Danny could fashion all sorts of wild things, using his little pocketknife to carve monsters and ogres and bloodthirsty insects. His rucksack was always filled with blocks of wood and bars of soap, just in case he imagined something to make.

"I suppose it was," Riley said, plopping down on the bed next to him. "Da said it was blowing so hard he couldn't stand up straight."

"Do you think our ma was selkie, like da says she was?"

"No," Riley said. His father had always been fond of telling fanciful tales of the night he'd met their mother. "And she wasn't a mermaid or a faerie, either. She was just our ma, only younger."

Riley missed those bedtime stories, filled with characters from Irish myths and legends. There had been time for them back when life was much different around the Quinn house. Before his father had been sacked from his job, before he'd decided to buy in to the Speckled Hound, an old pub in Ballykirk.

Long hours serving the local crowd and occasional tourists meant that Eamon and Maggie Quinn were never home to put their boys to bed. Riley's older sisters, Shanna and Claire, did all the cooking and cleaning around the small white-washed cottage. The boys took care of the garden and milked the cow and tended the chickens they kept.

"We should go out there," Riley said. "Let's see if the wind will knock us down like it did to Da."

"Will you two just lay off and go to sleep?" Kellan looked over from the book he was reading. "Blathering about the weather isn't going to change it. And if you go out there Da will whip your arse until you can't sit down."

Kellan was the eldest, and the most clever of the three. At age twelve, Kellan was almost a teenager and Riley and Danny usually deferred to him. But Kell had been a real puss-face lately. All he seemed to care about was school and exams and making his grades.

"Piss off," Riley muttered. "This is our room, too, and we can talk as long as we want."

Riley had never been much concerned about his schoolwork. Except when the music teacher, the beautiful Miss Delaney, came round to their room. He loved to sing and the days she brought instruments along, he was always the first to try them, able to play by ear in a matter of minutes.

She'd even lent him a fiddle, which he'd been teaching himself how to play, and she'd promised to bring a guitar once he'd mastered three tunes. But what he truly loved was the songs she taught—old Irish songs, children's songs and ballads and pub tunes. And then, she'd sing in the simple and sweet style called *Sean Nós,* her beautiful, clear voice ringing through the room, unaccompanied by instruments.

"Listen to that," he said, leaning closer to the window. "The storm is singing." He hummed along with the sound, then added words to the tune.

The only good that had come out of his parents' work at the Hound was that the five Quinn children were expected to help out on the weekends, which was when the pub hosted local musicians. Rather than dragging his feet to work, Riley arrived early so he could finish his tasks in time to sit in a dark corner of the pub and listen to the music.

Riley pushed away from the window and crawled into the bed he shared with Danny. "Don't worry," he whispered. "The storm can't get us."

"Sing me a song," Danny said, snuggling beneath the worn bedspread.

"What do you want to hear?" Riley asked.

"The barley song. I like that one."

"'The Wind That Shakes the Barley,' it's called." Riley sang the song softly. "'I sat within a valley green, I sat me with my true love. My sad heart strove to choose between, the old love and the new love.'"

"Why are there always girls in the songs?" Danny interrupted.

"I guess people like to hear about love," Riley said. He really didn't understand it, either. He would have preferred songs about battles or murder or even aliens. But most of the songs he knew were about love and sadness. And someone was always dying. "Da says if you can sing a sad tune, the lassies will love you."

"Go to sleep!" Kellan shouted.

"Feck off!" Riley and Danny said simultaneously. They started to laugh, then pulled the bedcovers over their heads.

"Stupid gits," Riley whispered.

"Sing the rest of the song," Danny begged.

Riley continued, the sound of the wind and rain his only accompaniment. He couldn't help but wonder if he'd ever like a girl enough to sing her a song. And if he did, would she follow him around the same way the girls followed Kellan?

Love was much easier to understand when it was words in a song than when it happened in real life.

1

THE LINE FOR Customs and Immigration snaked around the room and out the sliding glass doors into the hallway. Nan Galvin searched for a clock, not sure about the local time. Back home in Madison, Wisconsin, it was five in the morning. Here in Ireland, at Shannon Airport, it was… "Eleven o'clock," she murmured, catching sight of a clock on the wall.

She smiled to herself. Though she'd planned hundreds of exciting trips in her head and flipped through travel books during her lunch hours, this was the first time she'd actually gotten on a plane and flown across an ocean. Everything around her seemed exotic, from the shape of the trash cans to the voice over the loudspeaker to the signs written in Gaelic.

"I'm in Ireland," she said, smiling to herself.

The line moved and she pulled her luggage along with her, getting ever closer to the row of desks and dour-faced immigration officials.

Her mother had visited Ireland, the summer after her college graduation. Twenty-seven years ago, Laura

Daley had stepped off a plane, just as Nan had just done, ready to begin a wonderful adventure in the land of her ancestors. Nan could only imagine the young woman her mother had been. Laura Daley Galvin had died of cancer when Nan was eight.

This trip was a way to discover the other side of her, she'd decided. After her mother's death, she'd cared for her father, keeping house, excelling in her schoolwork, living at home while she attended college and after she took her first job. As time went on, she'd become more like him—a quiet homebody, satisfied to find adventure between the pages of a book rather than in the real world.

A year ago, she'd buried Jim Galvin beside her mother. But it was the discovery of a trunk full of her mother's memories that caused Nan to reevaluate the person she was. The contents provided a window into the woman Laura Daley Galvin had been—adventurous, curious, spontaneous. And a packet of letters revealed a lasting friendship with an Irish woman named Carey, a woman that Nan was determined to meet.

She'd decided to start saving for an adventure and, to her surprise, it had taken her only nine months to save enough for ten days in Ireland. What would she discover here? Would she have an adventure as her mother had? Was there anything left of Laura Daley inside of her?

Somewhere, outside the terminal, a driver was waiting for her, ready to whisk her away to the pretty little seaside town of Ballykirk in County Cork and the beautiful country cottage she'd rented over the internet. Nan glanced at the clock and winced. He'd been waiting for three hours.

"Next!"

Nan stepped up to the desk and slapped down her passport and the immigration form she'd completed on the plane.

"Tiernan Galvin?" the agent said.

She never used her Irish given name, mostly because no one in Wisconsin could pronounce it properly. So, she'd adopted her father's nickname for her—Nan. "Yes," she said. "Tiernan Galvin."

"Are you here on business or pleasure?" the woman asked.

Nan couldn't help but smile. Just the sound of the woman's Irish accent fired her imagination. Her mother had loved this land so much that she'd given her only child a strange Irish name. Maybe she'd even walked through this very same gate at Immigration. "I'm here on vacation," she said. "Pleasure."

"Are you visiting anyone in particular?"

"No one. Well, actually, his name is…" From her jacket pocket Nan pulled out the email she'd printed out and showed it to her. "His name is Riley Quinn. From Ballykirk. But I don't know him. I'm just staying in his family's house. Guesthouse. He's picking me up. At least he was supposed to three hours ago. The plane was late taking off and now this line has gone on forever. God, I hope he's still there."

The woman examined Nan's documents, then nodded.

"If you have anything to declare, go through the red

channel. If not, the green channel," she said. "And welcome to the Republic of Ireland. Enjoy your holiday."

"Thanks," Nan said. "I will."

She followed the green signs and walked out into the baggage claim area. When she found the correct carousel, her luggage was already making its way around on the conveyor. She grabbed her bag and hauled it onto the floor at her feet. Hoisting her carry-on bag to her shoulder, Nan started toward the exit, her suitcase rolling along behind her.

She passed by a line of drivers holding cards with names on them and she searched for hers. When she didn't find it, Nan walked outside into the late-morning sun.

A row of cabs waited at the curb but there were no other cars or drivers with signs for arriving passengers. Nan cursed softly. What was she supposed to do now? Renting a car was ridiculously expensive and well outside her budget. She'd already paid to use the car provided with the guesthouse.

Though the drive to Ballykirk might be a wonderful adventure, Nan wasn't sure she could steer and read a map at the same time while driving on the wrong side of the road. There was adventure and then there was adventure. She dragged her luggage over to the first cab in line and leaned into the passenger side window. "How much to go to Ballykirk?"

The driver regarded her with a scowl. "It's a two-hour round trip. About a hundred and forty kilometers. That would be two-hundred thirty euros."

"I only have American dollars," she said. "I haven't converted my money yet."

"Oh, I don't take dollars," he said. "Don't really know the conversion rates. You could convert your money inside, but those money changers are all a pack of thieves."

Nan sighed. "How about a credit card?"

He shook his head. "That I won't, dearie. Check one of the other lads, they might. Try the bus. Or you can hire a car."

"All right," she said. "Thanks."

This wasn't exactly the way she'd pictured the start of her vacation. She'd planned so carefully, right down to the last dollar and the last minute. Not only had her plane been late taking off from Chicago, but she'd also nearly missed her connection in New York. Then they'd had to wait three hours until a storm system passed before leaving New York. The meals on the transatlantic flight were barely edible and she'd been stuck beside a crying child for the entire trip to Shannon. And now she was hungry and had a headache that made any more stress difficult. She had Riley Quinn's phone number. She'd call and find out where he was. But first she'd have to get some change for the pay phone.

"Money first," she murmured to herself.

"Do you have a light?"

Nan turned to find a man standing behind her, an unlit cigarette between his lips. Her breath caught and she stepped back, her gaze fixed on his handsome face. This was exactly how she'd imagined Irish men…except for the cigarette, of course. He had shaggy dark hair and chiseled features and eyes that were so blue they were almost gray. The shadow of a week-old beard darkened his features, making him look a bit dangerous. "What?" she croaked.

"A light?" he repeated.

Faded jeans hugged his long legs, and a T-shirt and a leather jacket hid wide shoulders. Dangerous, she thought to herself. And wild. And slightly disreputable. Not the kind of man she was usually attracted to. So why had her breath suddenly left her body? "No," she murmured. "I—I don't smoke."

He groaned, shaking his head. "Oh, you're one of those."

"Those?"

He shook his head. "Americans. Now you're going to tell me all about the health hazards and how second-hand smoke affects everyone and how—"

"No!" she interrupted, insulted by his assumption. This always happened to her. People assumed that as a librarian, she was fussy and prudish and hyperorganized. But this man didn't know she was a librarian and still he was judging her.

She was on vacation. No one knew her here. She could be whoever and whatever she wanted and she didn't want to be that person who shushed students at the library and told them they couldn't have sex in the stacks. She wanted to be worldly and adventurous and maybe even a bit alluring. "I just don't carry matches because I don't smoke. And I rarely have need to start a campfire or...light some dynamite. And if you want to kill yourself, I'm not going to stand in your way."

He stared at her for a long moment, an odd look on his face, her attempt at humor falling flat. Then he chuckled. "Sorry. I'm a little touchy. I gave up the cigs a year ago but when I find myself getting irritated or tired, I go back to old habits." He broke the cigarette in half and tossed it to the curb.

"Isn't that littering?" she asked.

"I prefer to call it minding my health."

She stepped off the curb to pick up the discarded cigarette. But an instant later, he grabbed her arm and yanked her out of the way of a fast-approaching taxi. The taxi tires screeched and she screamed, slamming hard into his chest as she stumbled.

He held tight, pulling her away from the traffic, his body warm and hard with muscle. She drew a deep breath and the scent of his cologne teased at her nose. Though he was a complete stranger, she felt safe in his arms. In truth, she felt more than safe. She felt alive, every nerve in her body tingling with excitement.

"Careful now," he said, his voice soft, his concerned gaze scanning her face. "I can't be saving your life all the time. And it wouldn't do to get yourself killed your first day in Ireland."

Nan's heart fluttered. They were close enough to kiss. She could feel the warmth of his breath on her cheek. His gaze shifted and suddenly, she felt as if he could read her thoughts. Embarrassed, Nan pulled out of his embrace, straightening her jacket and trying to remain calm.

Though there'd been men in her life, she'd never felt such an immediate and intense reaction to any of them. But then, most of the men she dated didn't look like this one—drop-dead gorgeous. "Thank you," she said, forcing a smile.

"'Twas nothing any other Irishman wouldn't do for a beautiful lady," he teased, his brogue more exaggerated.

Nan glanced nervously down the line of cabs. Had he just called her beautiful? She'd always prided herself in an absolute objective assessment of her strengths and weaknesses, and *beautiful* was not a term she usually applied to her appearance. He was beautiful. She was ordinary.

"Are you looking to hire a cab?" he asked.

"Do you have a cab?" Maybe now that they'd struck up a conversation of sorts, he'd agree to take her to Ballykirk. "Is that taxi yours?" she said, pointing to a cab idling at the curb.

"No. The bloke who drives it just went inside to use the loo. I'm watching it for him, in exchange for that cig you made me toss." He paused. "Are you looking for a ride?"

Nan nodded. "Someone was supposed to meet me here, but I think he may have left. My plane was late."

"Husband?"

"No," Nan said.

"Fiancé?"

"No!"

"Boyfriend, then."

"No, just a ride."

"Well, then, my day has just taken a turn for the better. I'd be happy to give you a ride. I was supposed to pick up some old lady and drive her to Ballykirk, but she never showed."

Nan gasped. "That's where I want to go! What a coinci—" She stopped, then regarded him suspiciously. "Are you Riley Quinn?"

The grin faded and he raked his hand through his hair. "Oh, shite," he muttered. "I've stuck my foot in it now. You'd be Nan Galvin?"

"I would be her," Nan said. He assumed she was an old woman? What had she ever said or done that had given him that impression? "You were supposed to wait at baggage claim with a sign."

He held out his hands and shrugged. "I figured I'd recognize you when you came out. But you're not old. I expected some lady with white hair and spectacles and sensible shoes."

"Why, because I'm a librarian? That's just silly stereotyping and I—"

"No," he interrupted. "Well, partly. But there were… clues. You sounded old."

"We've never spoken. We've only emailed. How could you possibly guess my age from a few emails?"

"I don't know. You write old. And you just seemed so…"

"So what?"

"So…prissy. Not in a bad way, mind you. Your spelling was perfect and your emails were so organized and precise."

"They were not!" In truth, they probably were. Nan prided herself on proper grammar and spelling. It was a professional responsibility that spilled into her personal life.

"You requested that I provide a premium brand of toilet tissue. And that the house be clean of all insects, spiders and bugs, living and dead. I'd call that finicky. Besides, you said you'd wanted to visit the land of your ancestors before you died, so I put two and two together and came up with…well, definitely not you."

Nan held fast to her temper. It wouldn't do to make this man angry now. He was her only mode of transportation. "You did say you'd meet me at baggage claim. And you weren't there. That's all I'm saying."

"I got tired of waiting. I've been standing around here for two feckin' hours waiting on you."

"I was supposed to arrive *three* hours ago."

"Well, I was running late. I've got things to do today and I'm wasting my time searching for an old lady who doesn't exist. I have to get back to the pub."

"I'm sorry to keep you from your late-morning drinking," she snapped. Yes, he was sexy, but he also could be a bit of an ass.

"My family owns a pub," Riley explained. "I work there, along with my brothers."

"And you run a guesthouse?"

"It doesn't take much running, but, yes, I do that, too—plus lots of other things. Like driving demanding tourists home from the airport." He shook his head. "You could have told me you were a fine bit of stuff."

Though she should have been insulted, Nan's irritation suddenly vanished and she smiled reluctantly. "'Stuff'? What do you mean by that?"

"Don't act like you don't know what I'm saying," he replied. "You're beautiful, so don't get your knickers in a twist if I call you on it." Riley reached into his jacket pocket and pulled out a crumpled piece of paper, then handed it to her. "There's your name. Come on. Spilt milk. I'm in the car park." He grabbed her suitcase and started across the road. When she didn't follow, he turned around and strode back, grabbing her carry-on. "It's this way," he said. "Don't expect I'll carry you, too."

Nan followed him across the road, hurrying to catch up with his long strides. "Maybe you should have had that cigarette," she shouted. "Or maybe a big handful of mood elevators would help your negative attitude."

He laughed out loud. "Now, why would you say that? I've been nothing but pleasant since the moment we met."

"And I haven't?"

He sent her such a charming smile that Nan couldn't do much more than laugh herself. "You've been a darling," he said.

It was impossible to be angry with the man, no matter how irresponsible he might appear to be. "Be careful," she called as he hauled her suitcase up a set of steps. "That's brand-new luggage."

Giving her a long-suffering glare, he picked the suitcase up in his arms and continued up the stairwell. "Jaysus, what do you have in here?"

"I'm staying for ten days. I needed my things."

"And what might those things be?" he asked. "Construction supplies? I won't be asking you to build your own cottage."

"I had to bring shampoo and soap and lotion. And all my guidebooks. And I had to bring some things to eat, like peanut butter and my favorite kumquat preserves. And my special tea. I know you won't have those things here."

"They let you through with that?" he asked.

Nan stopped short, her hand clutching the railing. "What do you mean? Was I supposed to declare it? They said just meat and dairy products. And plants. The jars have never been opened and I—oh, no. Do you think they consider tea a plant?"

"Oh, I don't know. Here in Ireland, plants usually don't have leaves."

"I have to go back."

She reached for her suitcase, but he pulled it away and grabbed her arm. "Oh, no, you don't," he warned. "We're not going back inside."

"But I may have broken the law."

"So you're a criminal now. You're just going to have to live with the shame. Come on, Alice Capone, let's get the hell out of here before you find another way to waste my day."

"If I get in trouble, I'm going to blame you," Nan said.

"Oh, you'll be fine. It'll be a grand adventure, your life on the run from the Irish authorities. It's better than kissing the Blarney stone, you know."

"This is not how I imagined my vacation going," she murmured.

When they reached the first landing, Riley stopped and turned back to her. "I'm sorry if I've been acting like a wanker." He held out his hand and she grasped it. "We'll begin again. Hello, Miss Galvin. I'm Riley Quinn. Welcome to Ireland. I hope you enjoy your stay."

Nan smiled, staring down at their hands, so casually joined. He had beautiful hands, long, tapered fingers. So he was a nice guy at heart. "See, that wasn't so difficult." The warmth of his hand seeped into hers and she realized the attraction she'd first felt for him was still there, only multiplied. A tingle snaked up her arm. He was handsome and funny and even a bit chivalrous. If he could sing, he'd be the perfect man. "Thank you," she said.

He held on, a lot longer than she considered polite. His thumb gently stroked the back of her hand, turning a benign greeting into something almost sexual. She didn't really mind. It felt nice. "The car is just up here," he finally said, his voice soft, his gaze fixed on her face.

Nan tugged her hand away then stuck it in her jacket pocket for safekeeping. "Lead on," she said.

RILEY DOWNSHIFTED the car as they approached the interchange, then looked over his shoulder as he turned onto the roundabout. When another car nearly cut him off, he laid on the horn, cursing beneath his breath. He'd never make it back to the pub for the lunch rush, so why bother trying?

Nan was sitting stiffly in her seat, her eyes wide

and her hands folded on her lap as if she were praying. "Don't worry, I've never had a wreck."

"It's a…" She cleared her throat. "It's a feckin' miracle," she finished, imitating his Irish accent perfectly.

Her use of an Irish curse seemed so ridiculous coming from a proper little thing like her, he couldn't help but laugh. "There you go. You'll fit right in with a mouth like that."

She grinned. "When in Ireland…"

Gad, she was pretty, Riley mused. Not at all what he usually pictured when he thought of American women. He'd met a fair number of American students in pubs all over Ireland, but his image had been finely honed early in life, by old episodes of *Baywatch*—long blond hair, tight bodies and tanned skin. And breasts that seemed a lot larger than those provided by nature.

Nan was fresh and feisty, with a very simple, straightforward beauty. Her short-cropped black hair curled softly around her face and long, dark lashes ringed vivid green eyes. She was stubborn and opinionated, the kind of woman who would make charming her a tough go, even for the most experienced Casanova. But then, Riley enjoyed a challenge.

Though he had been anxious to get back to the pub, now that they were on their way, Riley decided to get off the expressway and enjoy the rest of the trip. The local roads back to Ballykirk provided a picturesque drive and he found himself wanting to spend a bit more time with Nan before delivering her to the cottage.

"So, you mentioned that your family had a pub. Do

you serve lunches there? I'm starving. The food on the plane was awful."

"Best lunch in all of Ballykirk," he said.

"Are you the cook?"

"No. I tend to the bar every now and then."

"You're a bartender."

"No. Actually, I make my living as a musician. I write songs and sing. At the Hound and at other pubs around Ireland."

"You sing," she said, as if surprised by the news. "Really? Are—are you famous?"

"Depends on what you consider famous. I'm no Elvis. But people know who I am. They come to see me. They buy my CDs. But I'm not planning a stadium tour anytime soon."

"Maybe I can come and hear you sing," she said.

"Maybe you can," Riley replied.

She sent him a smile that was so sweet, he wanted to reach out and touch her again. He clutched the wheel until his knuckles turned white, wondering why he found himself so attracted to the American. It wasn't just the fact that she was pretty in an unconventional way. There was a wide-eyed innocence about her that he found intriguing. Women her age were usually quite jaded, but not Nan. There wasn't a cynical bone in her body.

As they continued on to Ballykirk, Nan seemed fascinated by each new sight that passed by her window— the churches, the graveyards, the stone walls. When they rounded a curve in the road, Nan threw her arm out and grabbed his shoulder. "Stop!"

"What?" Riley slammed on the brakes and the car skidded. "Jaysus, did I hit something? What was it?"

"That," she said, pointing over him to a crumbling round tower. "It's a round tower. I saw these in my guidebooks. They're called…cloy—cloh—"

"They're called *cloictheach*."

"I didn't think they'd just be sitting out in the middle of a field. Do you think they give tours?"

"Nah. That one's just a ruin."

"Let's go," she said. "I want to see it up close."

He considered her request for a long moment. They were expecting him back at the pub, but his cousin Martin was behind the bar. He could do the job if Riley was late. "All right. I guess we could stop for a bit."

"I have to get my camera," she said, searching for the door handle. "It's in my bag."

He leaned over her seat and opened the door for her. She jumped out of the car and opened the rear door, then grabbed her carry-on and rummaged through it. When she'd retrieved the camera, she ran up to the drystone wall surrounding the field.

"I'm in Ireland," Nan shouted, throwing her arms out. "I want to see it all, starting right now." She pointed to the tower. "I want to see *that!*"

Riley shook his head. She might be a bit fussy at times, but she was also adorable. He followed her, holding her hand as she scrambled over the wall. They walked across the field, Nan staring up at the old stone structure. "Who takes care of this? Why hasn't anyone rebuilt this? How old is this one?" She threw questions at him, one after another, not waiting for an answer.

"We have these all over Ireland," he said. "There's one just a few kilometers from Ballykirk. It's bigger than this one. And you can climb up inside of it."

She pointed to the small window at the top of the crumbling tower. "Don't you wonder who might have lived here? Who sat at that window and stared out over all this beauty?"

"I doubt anyone ever lived here. They lived in the area around the tower. Some say these were bell towers. Like a warning system for the people who lived in the area or a way to call them to worship. They may have been used for defense. People would shut themselves inside if they were attacked."

She gently ran her hand over the rough stone wall and closed her eyes. Riley watched her, wondering if she was tired or if she was saying a prayer. "Are you all right?" he whispered.

Nan glanced over at him. "Yes," she murmured, nodding. "I'm just…all the life this tower has seen. Where I come from, the oldest building is maybe two hundred years old. This is ancient."

She looked so beautiful, the color in her cheeks high, her gaze bright with excitement, that he couldn't help himself. He bent close and brushed a kiss against her lips. She didn't move when he drew back, just stared up at him with wide eyes.

Nan finally drew a breath. "I—I should take a picture. Stand by the door and look…fierce."

He did as she asked and posed for five or six photos before he grew impatient with her suggestions for posing. "You don't need another photo of me," he finally said. "Let me take a photo of you."

She posed for him and he took his time, watching her through the viewfinder. He'd always been attracted to girls with long hair, but short hair suited Nan Galvin. It was playful and sexy and he could imagine burying his face in it when he hugged her.

"All right," he said, clicking the shutter. "Got it."

A tiny smile played at her lips. "I want to remember everything about this trip," she said softly. As they walked back to the car, she held the digital camera out to him. "That's a good one," she said, pointing to the tiny screen. "You look very handsome. Although, you'd look better if you shaved."

Riley slowed his pace as she continued to review the photos. Yes, she was undeniably attractive. And that sweet body, so slender and delicate, was just as intriguing as her pretty face. But she was also very odd, that one. He jogged to catch up to her and when they reached the car, he pulled her door open and waited for her to get inside.

She turned her gaze up to his and then held out her hand. "Thank you."

Riley was so surprised he wasn't sure what he ought to do. He took her fingers in his, deciding that a handshake wouldn't do. Slowly, he brought her hand up to his lips. "No need for thanks. I was happy to...do whatever it was that I did." The urge to kiss her again was overwhelming and Riley leaned closer. And then, without considering the consequences, he caught her waist between his hands and pulled her against his body.

Their first kiss had been borne of impulse, quick and fleeting, but this kiss was very carefully crafted. He gently explored her mouth, teasing with his tongue until she opened beneath the assault. She offered no resistance and though the kiss may have surprised her as much as it surprised him, she didn't back away. When he finally did, she blinked up at him, her hand still resting on his chest.

"Lovely," he murmured.

Nan cleared her throat and nodded nervously. "I think this is going to be a wonderful vacation," she said. She climbed into the car and Riley closed her door, then hurried around to the driver's side.

"Bloody hell," he muttered beneath his breath. "What are you doing? She didn't come to Ireland to snog with a culchie like you, ya daft prick." Still, she must have enjoyed it. She hadn't slapped him across the face or called him out for such a bold move or even tried to put an end to the kiss. And maybe, if the opportunity presented itself again, he'd give it another go.

When he got behind the wheel, Nan was peering out at the round tower, her eyes watery. Jaysus, this didn't bode well. Kissing her had made her cry. "Oh, now don't do that," he murmured. "I'm sorry. I shouldn't have kissed you. But I—"

"No," she said, laughing softly. "It wasn't the kiss. That was lovely. Very nice. Better than nice. Excellent."

"Then why are you crying?"

"I—I guess I'd like to think my mom might have been here when she visited Ireland years ago. She loved history. She might have visited this tower and put her hands on those very stones."

"Well, now you have a picture to show her."

"She died when I was eight," Nan said.

Silently cursing his stupidity, Riley turned the ignition and the car started. When it backfired, Nan jumped, pressing her hand to her heart and startling her out of her melancholy. "Nothing a tune-up won't cure," Riley said. "She's a dependable old banger. You won't have to worry. She'll get you wherever you want to go."

"You're lending me this car?" she asked.

"This is it," he said, giving the dashboard a pat.

"*What* is it?"

"This is a Fiat. A Cinquecento. She may be small, but she's got four wheels and an engine."

"She has a stick shift," she said. "Which would probably indicate the opposite gender. And I can't drive a stick shift."

"It's not rocket science," he said. "I can teach you in just a couple of minutes. Besides, this car barely uses any petrol. Though it does have an oil leak you'll have to mind."

Nan tipped her head back and covered her face with her hands. "So the car looks like it belongs to a family of clowns. Please, please tell me the guesthouse isn't a hovel made of sticks and mud in the middle of some swamp."

"Bog," he said. "We call it a bog. And the cottage is very cozy."

"Those photos you sent were real?"

"It's my childhood home. My brother Kellan has recently renovated it. He lives there now and again when he's come down from Dublin. And my sister Shanna decorated it. She likes old things—antiques. It's just as the photos show. Better even."

Nan took a ragged breath and nodded. "Okay. As long as the cottage is nice, I'll be fine."

He reached out and grabbed her hand, looking for any excuse to touch her again. "Feel better, then? No more tears?"

"I'm good," she replied.

They rode for a long time in silence, Riley searching his mind for a topic of conversation without appearing to snoop. He wanted to know everything about her. Was there a man in her life? Did she love him? Was she thinking about kissing him again? "You're a librarian. You must really like books."

"I love books," she said. "I always have. Every one you open is a window into a new world."

"Did you open a book about Ireland? Is that why you're here?"

Nan shifted to face him. "My mother came to Ireland when she was twenty-two. Right after she got out of college. I came here looking for her."

"That's a noble purpose," he said, hoping that the mention of her mother didn't restart the tears. For a girl who appeared so fragile on the outside, Nan Galvin was made of steel beneath. "I can't imagine losing my ma at such a young age. I'm sorry."

"Me, too," she said.

"But your father is still alive?"

Nan shook her head. "He died last spring. He was

older than my mother. He never remarried. I used to think it was my fault, that he was so consumed with raising me that he didn't have time for anything else. But once I got older, I realized he didn't find someone else because my mother was his one and only love. He just wanted to be with her." She glanced over at him. "Do you believe in that? That everyone has just one person they can love?"

It was a strange question to ask a total stranger, but then Nan never seemed to run out of questions. When she wanted information, she simply requested it. Riley could honestly say he'd never given the notion much thought. But she deserved an answer. "Sure. Why not? It would probably explain why I'm still single."

"I don't remember much about her," Nan continued. "She had red hair and green eyes and the softest hands. She was an art teacher. Her great-grandparents came from Ireland. I think that's why she named me Tiernan."

"It's a beautiful name. But I've never heard it used for a girl. It's usually a boy's name."

"I know," she said. "I looked it up. I guess she liked the way it sounded."

"So what else have you planned to see?" he asked.

"Everything in and around Ballykirk," Nan said.

"And why Ballykirk?"

"Because this is where my mother stayed twenty-seven years ago," she said.

"I wonder if anyone about town would remember her?" Riley asked.

"I hope so," she said softly. "I really hope so."

Her voice was so soft, so filled with faith that he had

to fight the impulse to stop the car and pull her into his arms and kiss her again. He'd always acted on his instincts, but this time, Riley decided to let his attraction to her simmer for a time. She'd booked the cottage for ten days.

He had plenty of time to woo her and he intended to take full advantage of any opportunity she offered.

BY THE TIME THEY neared Ballykirk, Nan had decided that Riley Quinn was the sexiest man she'd ever met. It wasn't only the dark good looks. He had an endearing combination of boyish charm and masculine confidence that she found completely irresistible. Though kissing a stranger was rather scandalous for her usually conservative approach to men, it wasn't difficult to understand her motives. He was just so kissable.

Her coworkers had teased her about vacation romances and Nan had laughed them off, but now she had to consider the possibility. She wasn't the same person she was at home. From the moment she set foot on Irish soil, she'd felt a sense of freedom. If she could kiss him after knowing him for an hour, what would happen after a day?

Though Nan had had a few long-term relationships in the past, she couldn't say she'd ever been in love. Perhaps her reluctance came from watching her father's loneliness increase with every year that passed. In her world, lost love had the capacity to bring a great deal of pain, sometimes lasting a lifetime. So she'd never taken the risk, never completely surrendered her heart.

As for Riley, his charms would only go so far. Even

if he was bent on kissing her again, she had no intention of falling in love with him. There was absolutely no future in it. But that didn't mean she couldn't enjoy a vacation romance.

As they raced down the country roads, Riley pointed out interesting sights and accompanied his travelogue with witty stories about the local folk. Irish music blared from the car's speakers and every now and then, he'd sing along, in a beautiful tenor voice.

As the warm August breeze blew through the open windows, Nan realized that she'd told the truth at the immigration desk. She was here for pleasure. But a different kind of pleasure—the kind that filled her senses, that made her body come alive and her mind open to new possibilities. The kind that only a man's touch might bring.

Nan had always read that Ireland was a land filled with magic and now she understood why. From the moment she stepped out of the airport, she felt as if she'd been carried into another world. All around her, the colors were brighter and the sounds more beautiful. The air smelled sweet and the man sitting beside her had captured her imagination.

As they reached the coastline, Nan got a good view of the water, the road running along the edge of the rugged, windswept hills. Every gothic novel she'd ever read came to mind and she imagined the heroines standing alone on the cliffs, their skirts buffeted by the ocean breeze.

"That's Ballykirk down there," Riley said, pointing

to a small gathering of whitewashed buildings on the waterfront.

But instead of continuing on to town, he turned up a narrow lane, taking her higher into the hills. "I thought the cottage would be closer to town," she said.

"It's not far," he said. "A brisk walk is all. And there are bicycles at the cottage. And you'll have the car."

"The car I can't drive," she said.

He glanced over at her and grinned. "Just point it down the hill and take your foot off the brake. You'll roll right into town."

"That's not funny."

"Let's get yourself settled and then I'll give you a lesson later this afternoon. You'll be tearing up the road in no time."

He made one more turn and a pretty thatched-roof cottage came into view, its whitewashed exterior bright in the noonday sun. Riley pulled the car to stop on the road, outside a low drystone wall that surrounded the front yard. "Here we are," he said. "Home sweet home."

Nan looked out, then turned to him and smiled. "It's so cute," she said, overwhelmed with both relief and delight. "It's so much prettier than the pictures." She hopped out of the car and walked up to the iron gate. A garden filled with colorful blooms flanked the narrow front walk and she drew a deep breath of the perfumed air. As she looked more closely, she saw little cast-iron animals, peeking from beneath low-lying leaves.

"Look at this," she said, bending down and pointing to one of the sculptures.

"Hedgehog," Riley said. "My brother makes those.

He has a blacksmith shop in town." He opened the trunk of the car. "Go on. The door is open. I'll bring your bags."

She ran up the walk, flung open the rough plank door and stepped inside. The entrance led into a simple living area with a worn wood floor. Rag rugs were scattered about and a huge hearth dominated one wall. Opposite the front door, and next to the back door, the kitchen was tucked into a small room with an adjoining bathroom. A collection of shabby chintz furniture, the colors a pretty contrast against the rough white walls, was gathered around the hearth.

Both bedrooms were tiny, but like the rest of the cottage, quaintly furnished. She circled around the old iron bed, her hand smoothing over the handmade quilt, then she threw open the window set in the thick wall. The breeze swept away the stuffy air and Nan fell back onto the bed, completely pleased with her surroundings. "It's perfect," she whispered.

"This used to be my room." Riley stepped through the doorway and placed her suitcase on the other side of the bed. "My brothers, Kellan and Danny, and me had this room, and my ma and da had the other. And my two sisters, Shanna and Claire, had the loft above us."

"It's cozy," she said. "I love it." She sniffed. "What's that smell?"

"Peat. We burn it in the hearth. The cottage doesn't have heat, but it's August so you shouldn't be chilly. But if you are, you can call down to the pub and I'll come up and start a fire for you. Or there are some portable heaters in the closet." He stood next to the bed, watching her, his hands shoved in his jean pockets. "I guess I'll leave you then. Unless you'd like to come down and have lunch. Your rent includes a meal a day. The pub serves lunch and dinner, but I could probably find you breakfast as well."

She circled around the bed, her hand running along the contours of the iron bed. "I think I'll unpack first. And then maybe take a nap."

"A kip," he said. "That's what we call it here."

"A kip," she said.

Riley chuckled. "There you go. Well, when you're ready, just follow the road down to the village and you'll find us at the end of the street right near the water. The Speckled Hound."

"All right. And later we'll have our driving lesson?"

"We will."

They stood, staring at each other silently for a long moment. Nan held her breath, wondering what was going through his mind. Was he thinking about kissing her again? And if he did, would she be able to keep herself from kissing him back? She waited, hoping he'd try. When he stepped toward her, she released her breath in a soft sigh.

"About what happened earlier…?" he murmured.

She nodded. "Uh-huh."

"I probably shouldn't have done that. I was just having some fun."

"You've kissed a lot of girls just for fun?"

He nodded slowly, his gaze still fixed on hers. "Yeah, I have."

"You're very good at it."

He chuckled softly. "I get my share of practice."

"And is there a girl—a special girl—that you kiss more often than other girls?" Nan asked. "Maybe one that you're going to be kissing for the rest of your life?"

Riley chuckled. "No. There was, but…"

His voice trailed off, leaving her curious. "But?"

"She took off a few years ago. She wanted a wee bit more out of life than a part-time barkeep and a singer with a mediocre voice could give her. She lives in Galway now with her husband."

"Then you're free to kiss anyone you want."

"That I am," Riley said. He took another step closer. "Would that be an invitation?"

Nan drew a deep breath. She wanted to scream her answer. *Yes! Kiss me again, throw me down on the bed, rip off my clothes.* "I'm not sure. If it was, would you accept it?"

"Well, why don't we just give it a try?" He reached out and smoothed his hands around her waist, then drew her closer. His mouth came down on hers, softly at first. And then his tongue traced a path along the edge of her lips and Nan opened her mouth, her tongue meeting his. She was already familiar with his taste, but she wasn't expecting the rush of desire that coursed through her.

Suddenly, the kiss wasn't enough. She wanted him to touch her, to pull her body against his, to overwhelm her with his own need. She splayed her fingers against his chest, his body all hard muscle beneath her touch.

It was obvious from the way he slowly seduced her with his mouth that he knew exactly what he was doing.

He kissed her exactly the way a woman would want to be kissed, deeply and romantically, and Nan did her best to keep up.

Riley turned her around and pressed her back against the wall of the bedroom, catching her hands and pinning them on either side of her head. Nan felt vulnerable, exposed, her desire evident in every ragged breath she took. Her heart slammed inside her chest, blood rushing through her veins and setting every nerve afire.

When he finally stepped back, she nearly collapsed onto the floor. She'd never really been kissed like that before. Was it an Irish thing? Did Irish men practice more than American men? Or had she just spent too much time with men who didn't really know what they were doing?

"Are you all right?" he asked.

She swallowed hard. "Yes."

He cupped her cheek in his hand. "I'm going to leave you now. I'll see you later?"

"Yes," she said. Strangely, one-word answers were all she could manage.

He gave her one last kiss, then strode out of the room. Nan stood numbly against the wall and listened as the car started outside. The sound of the engine faded into the distance and it was only then that she allowed herself to breathe normally.

Stumbling to the bed, she quickly sat down, clutching the quilt in her fingers as she tried to regain her composure. Oh, she'd had a lot of expectations for this vacation. But she'd never once dreamed that this would happen. She pressed her fingertips to her lips and closed her eyes, instantly recalling how incredible he was. Then with a groan, she flopped back on the bed and stared up at the ceiling.

Her mind was racing, trying to put order to her thoughts. This was how Heathcliff had kissed Cathy, how Rhett had kissed Scarlett. It was epic in its sheer sexual power. It was pure fantasy. And she wanted to experience it, again and again, until she'd had enough.

Was this why her mother had found Ireland so enchanting? Maybe Laura Daley had come to Ireland and had a wonderful romance, swept away by an Irish boy with dark hair and sexy blue eyes. And maybe they'd had to part, their desire impossible to satisfy with an ocean—and half a continent—between them.

Nan scrambled over the bed, crossing her legs in front of her, and rummaged through her carry-on. She found her camera and flipped it on, then held it at arm's length and took a picture of herself.

The photo came up on the display screen and she studied her image. She didn't look any different than she had when she left home yesterday. Her hair was still the same dark, short-cropped style, and her skin was still impossibly pale. Maybe she was just more attractive to Irish men than American men.

Her stomach growled and she pressed her hand to her belly. She should have been ready for a nap, ready to recover from a case of jet lag. But instead, Nan felt energized. She threw open her suitcase and pulled out her shampoo and soap. She'd take a shower, get dressed and walk down to the village for a late lunch—with Riley.

With a laugh, she jumped off the bed and stripped out of her clothes. "I love Ireland," she murmured. "And I adore Irish men."

2

"WHERE THE BLOODY HELL have you been?"

Riley tugged off his jacket and stepped behind the
bar. He grabbed an apron from the drawer and tied it
around his waist. His cousin Martin glared at him from
beneath a shock of spiked magenta hair. When he wasn't
hauling Riley's gear or setting up a show, the twenty-
two-year-old had worked at the pub and managed to find
something to complain about every day of the week.

It was well past the lunch rush and only a few patrons were still sitting inside the dimly lit pub. Riley
had decided to take a detour after dropping Nan off at
the cottage, grabbing a quick shower and shave at his
flat above the pub before coming downstairs.

"I told you, I had to run up to Shannon and pick up
that lady who booked the cottage."

"Your car's been parked out front all morning. How
did you get there?"

"I took the Fiat. I needed to buy new tires for it. You
made it through lunch on your own, so what's your
gripe?"

"My gripe is these three bastards sitting at the bar," he said, pointing to the Ballykirk barflies, affectionately known as the Unholy Trinity. "They got every last penny of me tips, shiftless eedjits."

"You know better than to gamble with them. They're notorious cheats. And you're far too gullible."

This caused a vigorous protest from the elderly trio—Markus Finn, Dealy Carmichael and Johnnie O'Malley. "Oh, change the boy's nappy there," Dealy teased. "He's nothing but a mewling babby, that one."

Riley held out his hand and wiggled his fingers. "Give it up, boys. I've never known you to play a game of chance without fixing the odds squarely in your direction. Was it the marked cards or the loaded dice?"

They reluctantly dug into their pockets and pulled out handfuls of coins and bills. Martin scooped up his tips and shoved them back in his apron, then wagged his finger at the old men. "You'll not be doin' that again. I won't fall for your tricks."

He strode off to the kitchen in a foul temper, the three men chuckling to themselves. "We've got to teach the boy," Johnnie said. "Every time you take Martin to Dublin, that band of yours robs him blind."

"Never mind the lad," Markus said, waving his hands. "Tell us about this lady you picked up, Riley. Dealy here has been suffering under a long, painful dry spell. Is she pretty? Or does she look like Johnnie's bulldog?"

"Dealy won't care," Johnnie said. "Without his eyeglasses, he'd fall in love with a milk cow. But he does like a girl with some meat on her bones."

"You don't know what I like," Dealy said. "And I don't need you watching out for my romantic interests."

Riley picked up a rag and wiped the wooden bar in front of them, picking up their half-finished pints of Guinness as he did. "I don't think she'll be interested in any of you bounders. She's young. My age. And far too pretty for the lot of you."

"Oh, now that makes things interesting, doesn't it, boys?" Markus crowed. "Riley, here, has a possibility. I don't believe he's had a possibility for four or five months. Who was his last possibility? That sweet little blonde from Glengarriff, wasn't it?"

"Oh, I remember her," Dealy said. "She was lovely. Beautiful breasts."

He was in a sad state when the entire town of Ballykirk knew the last time he'd bedded a woman. It wasn't as if he hadn't had opportunities. Being a musician had its advantages, especially when you worked late nights at pubs filled with drunken girls. But he just hadn't met anyone lately who interested him.

"You know, there is no law that says I have to serve you," Riley said. "If you insist on antagonizing the help here, I'll put you out on the street. Now finish your Guinness and get the hell out of my pub."

"Last time I looked, this was still your da's pub," Markus said.

"And we were just going to have ourselves a game or two of darts," Dealy said.

Riley sighed. The three pensioners spent most of their midday at the pub, sandwiched between fishing in the morning and endless games of dominoes outside the green grocer in the afternoon. The routine was repeated every day except Sunday, when they all went to church in the morning and spent their afternoons at family dinners with their grown children.

"If she comes in here, I expect you three to behave yourselves. There's no need for you to be telling tales for your own amusement."

"Well, what's she doin' here if she doesn't care to socialize?" Markus asked.

"She's here to see the sights. Her mother stayed in the village years ago and she's come to visit some of the same places."

The front door of the pub opened and they all turned to look. Riley straightened as he saw Nan step inside. She glanced around and when she spotted him, she smiled and waved.

"Now there. She's lovely," Dealy murmured. "Small breasts, but lovely."

"Look at her," Markus said. "She looks like Audrey feckin' Hepburn."

"Oh, the wife loves Audrey," Johnnie commented. "Seen all her movies." He cocked his head in Nan's direction. "What's her name, then?"

"Nan. Nan Galvin. Although her real name is Tiernan."

"That's a boy's name," Dealy whispered. "Why would anyone give a pretty thing like her a boy's name? They do that in America, you know. Some eedjits once named their daughter Moon Unit. Who the hell was that, Johnnie? Remember, we read it in the magazine?"

She crossed to the bar and sat down on a stool next

to the Unholy Trinity. "Am I too late for lunch?" she asked Riley.

Riley leaned over the bar, bracing his elbows on the scarred wood in front of her. "You surely aren't," he said.

It had only been an hour since he'd seen her, but she looked even prettier than he'd remembered. Her hair was damp and curled around her face and her color was high from the walk down the hill. His gaze dropped to her mouth, those lush lips that were so soft and warm beneath his. "What can I get you?" he asked.

"What do you have?" she countered.

Riley stifled a groan. Right now, the possibility of an embarrassing erection. How was it possible that the mere sight of her caused that kind of reaction, he wondered.

The three men watched the two them, nodding as their gazes darted back and forth between Riley and Nan. Conversation would be impossible with three overly interested eavesdroppers. Never mind that the entire village would know the details of the conversation before the end of the day, but they'd no doubt interrupt with questions of their own.

"Aren't you three late for a game of dominoes?" he asked, giving them a pointed glare.

For a moment, they protested, then realized what Riley was getting at. They quickly jumped up and headed to the door, chatting as they left. Once the door shut behind them, the pub was empty—and quiet. Riley stepped out from behind the bar and walked to the door.

After flipping the lock, he dropped the Closed sign in the window.

"Do you always encourage your customers to leave?" Nan asked. "It's a wonder you've been able to stay in business."

"Unless you want to reveal your darkest secrets to all of County Cork, you should be happy I sent them out," Riley said, returning to his spot opposite her. He drew Nan a half pint of Guinness and set it in front of her, then circled the bar to sit down next to her. He turned her to face him, trapping her knees between his and smoothing his hands over her thighs. "So, tell me all your deepest and darkest secrets. What do you like to eat for lunch?"

She picked up her Guinness and took a sip, then wrinkled her nose. "I'm a salad girl," she said.

"Try the Guinness again," he said. "It's an acquired taste."

She took another sip. "What kind of salads do you have?"

"Katie!" A few seconds later, the pub's cook stepped out of the kitchen. "What kind of salads do we have today?"

"We don't have salads," she said. "We've got shepherd's pie, bangers and mash, and corned beef with cabbage and red potatoes. And I've a bit of seafood chowder left."

"The chowder sounds great," Nan said. She watched Katie return to the kitchen, then glanced around the pub. "You said your parents owned the pub. Are they here?"

"They're off caravanning." He caught her quizzical

look. "What? Caravanning? They have a big caravan and they drive it places and camp—"

"Oh," she said. "An R.V.? A recreational vehicle. A little home on wheels?"

"Yes. They'll be back in September and then I get back to my regular dissolute life. As a musician, I spend my days writing impossibly bad lyrics and trite tunes and my evenings trying to sing them."

"I thought you'd cut your own CDs. Are you really that bad?"

"Only in my own mind," he said with a chuckle. "I make a decent living. I'll never be a millionaire, but I pay my bills. And I love what I do."

He'd always enjoyed the fact that his profession came with scads of female admirers, a benefit he'd taken advantage of on many occasions. But Riley suspected Nan was not the kind of girl who jumped into bed with a guy just because he played a guitar and sang a pretty song.

"And you sing here?"

"Every Saturday night throughout the summer," he said. "You'll have to come see me."

"I'd expect you have a lot of girls coming to see you," Nan said.

"Not a one as pretty as you are, Nan Galvin." He leaned forward to steal a kiss, but before he could, Katie barged through the kitchen door. He waited while she put the crock of soup in front of Nan, along with a plate of sliced homemade bread and butter.

"Thank you," Nan said, giving her a smile.

"Cherry tart for dessert," she said. "Warm from the oven. Can I get you a piece?"

She grinned. "All right. I'm famished. Bring it on."

"That's the spirit," Katie said, walking over to the kitchen door.

Nan dug into the chowder, then groaned. "It's wonderful. This place is wonderful. It's exactly how I'd imagined an Irish pub to be," she said.

"Now, I know you have pubs in America," he said.

"I don't spend a lot of time in them," she said. Nan pointed to a pair of socks hanging from a rafter. "I'm sure there's a good story behind those."

"There's a hundred years of stories in this pub," he said. "The Speckled Hound has been around since the turn of the nineteenth century. I don't know them all. But I do know one." He grabbed her hand and drew her along to a dark corner. "There was this pretty American girl who came to Ballykirk and she walked into the Speckled Hound and the bloke behind the bar was so besotted that he had to kiss her."

"Besotted?" Nan asked.

"Yeah, besotted." He bent close and captured her mouth, his hands spanning her narrow waist. He dragged her off the stool and trapped her against the bar, his hands braced on either side of her. A current of desire raced through his body as her fingers furrowed through the hair at the nape of his neck. This wasn't just some one-sided infatuation, Riley thought to himself. She was kissing him back, her tongue tangling with his, her hands wandering over his body.

The taste of her was like a drug, so incredibly addictive that all he could think about was more. He ran his palms along her waist and then slipped them beneath her shirt, searching for warm, smooth flesh.

Riley couldn't remember the last time he'd felt the need to completely possess a woman. Most of the women he'd been with the past few years had been nothing more than physical attractions, driven by a hot body and raw need. The truth was, he hadn't wanted anything more than that.

But this was different. He wanted to know everything about her—what she loved, how she lived, all the tiny details that made her the fascinating woman she was. Still, he wondered if the attraction was intensified because the clock was ticking. She'd leave in ten days and he'd never see her again. Was that the source of his desire?

"I've never kissed an American before," he murmured, his lips barely touching hers. "I don't think I realized what I was missing."

She smiled, then pulled him into another kiss. "This is not what I expected when I told the immigration officer I was here for pleasure."

"Oh, that I can provide." He nuzzled his face into the curve of her neck. She smelled so good. He'd almost forgotten how nice it was to have a woman to focus on, even if it was only temporary. "Why don't you finish your lunch and then we'll go out for a drive. I have a place I'd like to show you."

He wrapped his hands around her waist and set her back on the stool. She picked up her spoon. "This is really good. I didn't realize how hungry I was."

Riley watched her eat. Unlike some of the girls he'd

known, she seemed to enjoy her food. He hated to see a woman pick at her food like a bird. "So, I think we should go out tonight. Find some fun."

"Are you asking me on a date?"

"Yeah. Why not? It's your first night in Ireland. I think I should try to make it memorable."

"All right. It's a date," she said.

Riley grinned. Now all he had to do was convince Danny to work at the pub tonight—and if things went well, for the next ten days.

"Now, let the clutch out very slowly and at the same time, give it a bit of…I think you'd call it gas."

Nan focused on Riley's instructions. She'd been behind the wheel for nearly a half hour and managed to drive no more than five or ten yards at best, and that was on a completely flat road. "All right. Slowly. Slowly," she said. The car stopped with a jerk, the engine dying. "And I'm going to ruin your car in the process. This can't be good for it." She turned to Riley. "Are there no cars in Ireland with an automatic transmission?"

"Of course there are. I just don't happen to own one. So this car will have to do, unless you plan to see Ireland by bicycle or on foot."

She drew a deep breath. "All right. One more time. But if I kill it again, we're done. At least for now."

"Crossed fingers," Riley said. "Just a nice smooth switch, one pedal out, then the other in. Feel where the clutch catches."

She did as she was told, focusing on the clutch as she let it out. And suddenly, she realized what he was talking about. She felt the clutch engage and gave the car a bit of gas. To her astonishment, they started off down the road, the ride smooth.

"Oh, my God!" Nan cried. "I'm doing it. I'm driving in Ireland. I'm driving in Ireland."

"All right, now let's shift."

"No, no, no. Let's just stay at this speed."

"Nan, we can't drive in first gear forever. Shifting isn't hard once you get going. Just push the clutch in, shift and let it out slowly." He put his hand over hers on the gearshift. "Ready?"

Nan winced. "Ready."

"Clutch in. Shift. Clutch out. And there we go."

She laughed. "All right, now we're moving. This isn't so hard. What's next?"

"Third gear," he said. "Speed up a little. Clutch in. And shift. Clutch out."

They rolled along on the deserted road, Nan's mind spinning with all the things she had to remember. The steering wheel was on the wrong side of the car and the car was on the wrong side of the road. And she had three pedals where there were usually two. And the gearshift made things nearly impossible. But now that she could drive, her adventures could begin.

The truth was, as long as she couldn't drive, Riley would be required to accompany her wherever she wanted to go. "Stop sign," she said, pointing down the road. "Stop sign!"

"Don't worry. Just do what you do in your car. Take your foot off the accelerator and put it on the brake."

To her relief, the car began to slow as it approached the stop sign. But then it began to shudder.

"Clutch in, clutch in," he said.

But she wasn't quick enough and the engine died. They slowly rolled up to the stop sign, the car silent. "I think this would be a good place to stop for today," she said.

He slipped his arm around her shoulders. "You did a fine job of work there. A few more lessons and you'll be ready to go solo. Until you're ready, I'll drive you wherever you want to go."

Nan smiled. "Don't you have to work?"

"Nah, my brother Danny is going to work for me. He's barely worked all summer, so he owes me some time." Riley reached over and grabbed her waist. "Come on, let's switch." He pulled her on top of him, wriggling toward the driver's seat.

But the car was ridiculously small and their limbs tangled together until it was impossible to move. "Now I know how those clowns feel," she said, laughing.

"Wait," Riley said. "You're coming very close to un-manning me."

"You're the one who wanted to do this!" Nan cried. "We could have used the doors like normal people."

"Oh, but it wouldn't have been half as much fun." Riley finally pulled her legs on either side of his hips. His face was pressed into the side of her chest. "I think maybe we should rest for a bit," he murmured. "Just like this."

"Why do I get the idea that you planned this?"

"Oh, I think this is one of those happy accidents,"

he said. "And now that you're here, what are we going to do with ourselves?"

Nan felt her left leg cramping and she stretched it out. But as soon as she did, the car began to roll. "We're moving," she said.

He looked out the window. "Is your foot on the clutch?"

"I don't know. I can't see my foot."

They twisted around, Riley trying to get into the driver's seat. Nan screamed as the car continued to roll.

"Ow," Riley shouted as she kneed him in the groin.

"Sorry, sorry."

When he finally settled in the driver's seat, he pulled the emergency brake and the car stopped. Cursing softly, he shoved the door open and stepped out of the car, then circled around it and pulled open her door.

"What? I'm not driving again."

He reached in and took her arm, gently drawing her out of her seat. But the moment she stood, he yanked her into his arms and into a long, desperate kiss.

Nan leaned back against the car, surrendering to the feel of his mouth on hers. His hands moved over her body, sending shivers coursing through her. She arched against him as her instincts took control, the need to get closer overwhelming her senses.

They'd known each other for less than a day and yet this kissing had become almost second nature. Pleasure was the only objective and any inhibitions she might have had were gone. She wanted him to touch her, to kiss her, to completely possess her body. She wanted him to strip off her clothes and wrap her legs around his waist and bury himself deep inside her. All these thoughts came rushing forth, shocking her, yet piquing her desire at the same time.

Her pulse pounded and adrenaline rushed through her body. She grabbed the hem of his T-shirt and pulled it up, running her hands beneath the soft fabric. His chest was smooth and muscular, a soft line of hair running between his collarbone and his belly.

The kiss continued to deepen, but then he broke away. Riley slid down in front of her. He pressed his face to her belly, then slipped her shirt up, trailing kisses across her torso. His palm found the soft swell of her breast and Nan moaned as he ran his thumb over her nipple.

A moment later, he was back at her mouth, kissing her as if he couldn't seem to stop. She felt weak and powerful all at once—unable to resist yet certain of how much he wanted her. Was it even necessary to slow things down? Or could they just admit where this was heading?

He leaned into her and she could feel his desire, the hard ridge of his erection evident through the faded fabric of his jeans. Nan fought the urge to touch him there, but her curiosity got the better of her. She smoothed her hands over his belly and then moved lower.

His breath caught in his throat and then he growled softly, cupping her face in his hands. "What are you doing there?" he murmured. "Trying to drive me completely around the bend?"

"I'm just having a bit of fun," she teased. Nan glanced up at him. "Would you like me to stop?"

"I think that would be best for now. But I reserve the right to continue on later." He looked around, then gave her a quick kiss. "Come on. If we don't hurry, we're going to miss the sunset."

They got back in the car, this time with Riley behind the wheel, then headed down the coast road. Nan was no longer interested in the landscape passing by, beautiful as it was. She couldn't seem to keep her eyes off of Riley. How could a man as beautiful as he was find her desirable?

It had to be the fact that she was American. To him, that meant exotic and men always preferred exotic to ordinary. Or maybe she just looked like someone who would be easy to seduce. Having a vacation affair was much simpler than dealing with a real relationship. Ten days and it was done.

In truth, it really didn't make a difference why Riley was attracted to her. She wasn't going to question his desires, especially when hers were just as strong. She'd come to Ireland to lose herself in new experiences, to find an adventure. A passionate affair with Riley Quinn was exactly what she wanted.

The little Fiat headed down a steep hill, then up a rise. Nan glanced out the window, then sucked in a sharp breath. "Oh, my God." She looked over at Riley. "It's stunning."

He nodded. "I thought it would be good tonight. There were just enough clouds on the horizon to make it grand." He pulled the car off the edge of the road. "Let's go get a better look."

They followed a footpath to the top of the rise. Below them, the Atlantic crashed against the rugged shore and far out on the horizon, the setting sun had lit the sky ablaze with brilliant pinks and oranges. Soft streaks of color shot into the deep blue sky, nearly touching the first stars that twinkled above them.

"It's not often like this," he said. "But when it is, it's always spectacular."

Nan wrapped her arms around his waist and hugged him. Furrowing his hand through her hair, he kissed the top of her head. She felt so incredibly alive standing here with him, all of her senses overwhelmed by him. She was still Nan Galvin, but a better version of herself, a woman comfortable with pleasure. Was this what her mother had experienced?

"What's the name of this place?" she asked.

"Cod's Head," he said. "That's Ballydonegan Bay. And out there is Dursey Island." He pointed straight out to sea, to a spot near the sun. "And over there is America. Where you came from."

Home seemed so far away; not just geographically, but emotionally, Nan thought to herself. Since her father had died, she'd felt so alone in her quiet, empty house. Maybe it wasn't a surprise that Ireland felt comfortable. It was part of her DNA and half of her family history.

"I need to do something while I'm here," Nan said. "And I may need some help."

"Name it," he said.

"Not too long ago, after my father died, I was going

through some things in the attic. I found a box of my mother's things and inside, there was a packet of letters from Ireland. For years, from the time she left Ireland until she died, she carried on a correspondence with someone named Carey."

"Is that his Christian name?"

Nan blinked, surprised by his question. "Then it would be a man? I thought maybe Carey was a woman?"

"Could be either," Riley said.

"She must have talked about me in the letters because this Carey always thanked her for the news. And my mother sent pictures, too. That's why I thought she was a woman. Maybe a good friend she met on her trip? She could even be a distant relative. But she lives in Bal-lykirk, or at least she did twenty-seven years ago." Nan looked up at Riley. "I want to find her. I want to know what my mother was like when she was my age."

"Is that important?"

"There are so many conversations that we never had a chance to have," Nan said. "And I know so little about her. My father didn't like to talk about her, so I didn't bring the subject up. And her parents died when I was a teenager and I never really had the courage to ask them before that. I don't know why, but I have to know everything I can. And after reading the letters, Ireland was the best place to start."

"Do you have an old address?"

"There was only just the name of the town. I assumed that the town was small and the postmaster probably knew everyone."

"Tomorrow, after breakfast, we'll go ask at the post. That's a fine place to start."

"You don't think it's impossible, then?"

"Ireland is different from the States," Riley said. "People usually stay closer to home."

"I have ten days to find her," Nan said. And ten days to find herself. Who would she be when she got on the plane to go home? And how would her life change after that? A tiny sliver of fear shot through her, but she brushed it aside.

Adventure sometimes came with risks, but for the first time in her life, she wanted to take those risks.

AFTER WATCHING the sunset, they'd taken a long drive along the coast of the Kenmare, then drove along the river valley to Glengarriff, where they stopped for dinner. For Riley, it had been the perfect first date, full of conversation and laughter.

He hadn't wanted it to end but he knew as soon as he took her home it would probably be over. He wasn't sure she'd ask him to stay. They barely knew each other. And though she enjoyed kissing him and touching him, that might be where it all stopped. In an attempt to prolong the night, he decided to take her back to the Hound.

The pub was busy for a Monday night. The boys from the local rugby team had decided to stop by for a pint after their match and had brought their opponents with them. A couple of the lads had invited Nan to play darts with them and she'd happily agreed.

Riley watched her from across the pub, ready to rescue her if any of the boys got bold with her. She seemed to be having fun, but every now and then she'd glance his way and smile, as if they shared a secret.

"She's a pretty young thing," Danny said, leaning over the bar. "Where'd you find her?"

"She's staying in the cottage," he said.

"I thought you said some old lady had let the place."

"I was wrong."

"Well, now, there's a lucky mistake. Just watch yourself, boyo. It's wouldn't do to fall in love with her. Americans always go home."

"I know," Riley said, nodding. He took a long sip of his ale then noticed the group around the dartboards getting a bit rowdier than before. "I think it's time to take her home. Before they all start drooling on her."

As he wove his way through the patrons, Riley couldn't help but wonder just what he was doing. Danny was right. Nan would be leaving in ten days. Falling in love with her would be an exercise in futility. But holding back his affections wouldn't be right, either. He wanted to surrender to this crazy infatuation and see where it led. And if it led to sadness in the end, then he could handle it.

When Riley reached the group, he slipped his arm around Nan's shoulder and whispered in her ear. "Come on. Let's get out of here."

"Up the yard, Quinn!" the boys shouted. "We're in the middle of a tournament here. You can't steal our star player away now."

"Get back, you shower of savages," Riley teased, pushing them aside. "She's had enough of you warped eedjits."

"Not without a fight, we won't," Donal Duffy said, stepping forward and raising his fists.

"I'm not going to fight you," Riley said. He turned to see a fearful expression on Nan's face. "He's just joking."

Donal puffed out his chest. "No fists. We'll sing her a song and you sing her a song. She chooses the winner. And if she chooses us, she stays until the end of our little tournament."

The rest of the boys got behind the scheme, lining themselves up and clearing their throats. "You really think you can beat me?" Riley said.

"The way I hear it, you're not all that good," Donal said.

"All right. You're asking for a pint of humiliation, Donal Duffy. But I accept your challenge."

Donal stood in front of his mates and began the verse of "Wild Rover," a well-known pub song. As soon as he sang the first note, Riley knew he had him beat. What woman wanted to hear a drinking song?

"'I've been a wild rover for many the year,'" Donal sang in a decent baritone voice, "'and I spent all me money on whiskey and beer, and now I'm returning with gold in great store, and I never will play the wild rover no more.'"

The team joined him in the chorus, belting out the words with drunken glee, stomping to accent some of the words. "'And it's no, nay, never! No, nay, never, no more, will I play the wild rover. No, nay, never, no more!'"

The song went on for three more verses before it

ended in a raucous finish that included a bit of dancing and some out-of-tune harmonies. When it was over,
Nan clapped along with the crowd and congratulated
the singers on a job well done. Then she leaned close to
Riley and whispered in his ear. "Please tell me you have
something better. I'm tired and I want to go home."

"All right," Riley said, holding out his hands to quiet
the crowd. "This is an old song but one that's perfect
for the moment."

"Oh, Jaysus, please tell me he's not going to sing 'I
Love You, I Do,'" Donal muttered.

Riley smiled smugly. Everyone in Cork knew Riley
had written the pop hit, a silly little ballad that had paid
a tidy sum in royalties for the past five years. One of
Britain's most popular boy bands had recorded it, and
when it hit the top of the charts, Riley had become a
local celebrity. Unfortunately, it instantly became his
most requested number whenever he performed.

He grabbed a chair and put it in front of him, then
lifted Nan to stand on it. "I won't be singing that song,"
he muttered. The patrons grew silent as they waited
for him to start. Standing in front of her, Riley began
to sing the first verse of "Parting Glass," a traditional
Irish tune about saying farewell.

"Of all the money e'er I had, I spent it in good
company.
And all the harm I've ever done, alas, it was to
none but me.
And all I've done for want of wit to mem'ry now
I can't recall.

So fill to me the parting glass, good night and joy
be with you all."

Nan stared down at him, a smile playing on her lips,
her eyes shining. He sang the second verse to the crowd,
turning to the boys as the words turned to friendship.
But for the last verse, he turned back to Nan. Summoning up all the emotion he could find, he took her hands
and sang from his heart.

"If I had money enough to spend, and leisure time
to sit a while,
There is a fair maid in this town, that sorely has
my heart beguiled.
Her rosy cheeks and ruby lips, I own she has my
heart in thrall.
Then fill to me the parting glass, good night and
joy be with you all."

The crowd was silent for a long time after he ended.
Nan's eyes were teary and when she jumped off the
chair and threw herself into his arms, everyone erupted
in applause. The sound of their cheers faded as Riley
kissed her, his fingers tangling in her hair as he molded
her mouth to his.

"So, I guess that means I won?" he murmured, looking down into her eyes.

"Take me home," she said.

"That I will," Riley said, the turned to shake Donal's
hand. "Good song."

"Ah, I should have known better," Donal muttered. "Ye even brought a tear to my eye."

Riley wove his fingers through Nan's, then drew her along to the door. When they got outside, they strolled up the street to where they'd parked the car.

"That song was beautiful," Nan said softly.

"I sang it for you."

"No one's ever sung a song for me before."

They stopped beside the car. "Well, I had to make it good," Riley replied. "I was getting a bit tired of sharing you with those lads."

He pulled open the door and waited till she was inside, then circled to the driver's door. They drove out of the village and up the narrow road to the cottage. She hadn't left a light burning, so he held tight to her hand as they walked up the dark front path. When they reached the door, she turned and faced him.

"Thank you for today. For everything you did to make my first day in Ireland memorable."

He bent close and touched his lips to hers. "Glad to be of service," he murmured. "Is there anything else I can do for you?"

She opened the door behind her and backed inside, pulling him along with her. "You could help me find the lights," she said.

He reached around the door and flipped the lights on in the parlor. "How's that?"

"Better," she said.

With every moment that passed, Riley found himself more determined to deny his need. They'd barely known each other twelve hours and all he could think about was pulling her into the bedroom and getting them both naked. He'd even put a few johnnies in his wallet just in case he needed them. "You'll be all right up here by yourself?"

"Yes," Nan said, nodding.

"I could stay a little longer, if it would make you feel more comfortable." He slipped his arm around her waist and bent close to kiss her. It had almost become second nature, covering her sweet mouth with his, feeling her body in his arms.

As his tongue traced the crease of her lips, Nan sighed. She slipped her hands beneath the front of his jacket, pushing it over his shoulders. Riley tugged it off his wrists and let it drop to the floor. "I guess I'm going to be staying for a while?"

"A little while," she said with a smile. She shrugged out of her own jacket, then drew him along to the sofa. "I don't have anything to offer you to drink."

"I'm not thirsty," he said.

The need between them was growing with every fleeting touch. He sat down on the sofa, then pulled her down into his lap. Riley drew her mouth to his, hungry for her taste, his tongue plunging deep.

She tugged at his T-shirt and with a soft curse he pulled it off over his head and threw it aside. Her hands were all over him as he kissed her, smoothing over his shoulders, running down his chest. The sensation of her fingertips on his skin sent a flood of desire rushing through him.

He was already hard, his response to her instant and intense. She shifted on his lap and he groaned softly.

It was clear that she took the sound for impatience and Nan quickly discarded her own shirt, leaving her in just a lacy scrap of a bra.

Riley pressed his lips to the curve of her neck, then slowly moved lower, his tongue trailing over silken skin. When he reached the tops of her breasts, he tugged the lace aside, revealing the soft swell of flesh.

Nan raked her hands through his hair and tipped her head back, moaning softly as his tongue teased at her nipple, drawing it to a tight peak. Riley knew if he didn't stop now, there would be no stopping at all.

Nan wasn't just some girl he'd picked up after a show, someone he'd enjoy then never see again. She was someone he genuinely liked, someone he wanted to spend time with. And he wasn't willing to do anything to jeopardize that.

Slipping his arm beneath her knees, he stood up and carried her into the bedroom. The room was dark and cold, the breeze from the sea blowing through the open window. He gently laid her on the bed, then sat down beside her, bracing his hand on the other side of her body and leaning close.

"I'm going to leave," he said, dropping a kiss on her lips. "I don't want to, but I think it's probably a good idea. You need to get some sleep."

"I want you to stay," she said, reaching out to smooth her palm over his cheek.

"We've known each other for about twelve hours," he said. "I think maybe we should wait for another twelve to twenty-four before we sleep together…?"

She smiled. "All right."

"No one will ever accuse me of not being a gentleman," Riley teased.

"I already know you're not a gentleman," she said. "You called me prissy."

"Well, I was wrong, Miss Galvin. You're the most unprissiest woman I've ever met." He bent close again and kissed her. "I'll see you in the morning. Come down to the pub and I'll make us both breakfast."

He stood up and walked to the bedroom door, then turned back to her. "Good night, Nan."

"'Night, Riley."

Riley walked through the cottage and out the front door, into the cool night. He drew a deep breath and smiled to himself. He'd never in his life turned down a warm and willing woman. But then, he'd never wanted a woman as much as he wanted Nan. The best things in life were always worth waiting for.

3

"MORNIN'."

Nan smiled at the handsome man behind the bar, then realized he was the brother she'd met last night, freshly shaved and sober. "You're Danny, right?"

He nodded. "Danny. We met last night. Although it was so black in here that we didn't have time for a proper introduction." He held out his hand over the bar. "Danny Quinn. I'm the younger. Don't know if you'll get a chance to meet Kellan. He's the elder."

She shook his hand, then took a seat on one of the stools. "I'm Nan. Nan Galvin."

"I remember," he said, his smile wide. "And how are you enjoying your stay in Ballykirk so far?"

"I haven't seen much," she replied. "Riley said we were going out sightseeing after breakfast, but it's almost time for lunch. Is he here?"

"He had to make a quick run into Glengarriff to pick up mussels, but he said to tell you he'd be back around eleven. Which means, he'll be back in ten minutes. Can I get you anything while you wait?"

"Coffee, if you have it," she said, stifling a yawn. "I'm trying to reset my clock and I think it might take more than a day."

"How do you have it?"

"Black," she said. "And very strong."

"Katie's made some lovely soda bread. Can I interest you in a slice? Fresh out of the oven."

Nan nodded. "I'd like to try that. I read in my guidebook that it's traditional Irish food."

Danny disappeared into the kitchen. While she waited, Nan took in more details of the pub. She hadn't had much chance to really look around. Riley had told her about watching the singers in his parents' pub, about how he'd memorize all the songs and then try to figure them out on an old guitar his father had bought him.

This place was as familiar to him as the library was to her. She peered at an old photo hung above the cash register and then circled the bar to take a closer look.

A man and woman stood in front of the pub with two teenage girls and a trio of young boys. Nothing had changed much in the ensuing years with respect to Riley and Danny, Nan thought. The two Quinn brothers she'd already met still possessed their boyish smiles and tousled hair. The sisters, though all arms and legs, were already beauties.

The kitchen door opened and Danny reappeared with a plate and a mug. "Here we are," he said.

"I'm sorry," Nan murmured. "I was just taking a look at this photo. You and your brother haven't changed much."

"That was taken the day my da bought in to the

Hound," he said. "I think I was seven. Riley was nine and Kellan would have been eleven. Shanna and Claire were teenagers." He set the plate and mug on the bar. "There are other photos over on that wall. A few of Riley performing when he was just a lad."

She returned to her seat and picked up the coffee, then took a slow sip. "Umm, I really needed this. I have to shop for groceries today. I don't have anything up at the cottage. Where would I go?"

"We have a small green grocer in town. He sells locally grown vegetables. And the baker's right next door to him. If you want fish, just walk down to the waterfront when the boats come in. If you want chicken, Bobby Rankin raises them and will deliver them to the green grocer the day after you order. Anything else, you'll need a real supermarket and that's in Kenmare, across the pass."

"Thank you," she said.

"No problem," he said with a warm smile. "Now, you'll have to pardon me because I need to change out the barrel on the Guinness."

As promised, the soda bread was lovely—a bit tangy and filled with plump, sweet raisins. She spread butter over a slice and took a big bite, then groaned softly. It was the perfect breakfast food, she mused. Grabbing her mug, Nan walked over to the wall of photos, curious to find more of Riley. There were layers upon layers, some so old they were yellow and curled and the color faded.

As promised, there were a number of Riley performing at the pub, from the time he was just a young boy through adulthood. She compared each one, noting how happy he looked standing in front of the microphone, his guitar almost bigger than he was.

As she turned away to return to the bar, a snapshot caught her eye. Nan stepped closer, leaning in to the group of six young twenty-somethings—three men and three women. For a moment, her heart stopped beating and she felt dizzy.

One of the girls in the photo looked so much like her mother it was—no, it had to be her mother. She set her bread and coffee down on the edge of the pool table and carefully peeled the photo off the wall. Nan hurried over to the window, searching for more light.

"Oh, it is," she murmured, the words coming out on a sigh. There was no doubt in her mind. Though the colors were faded, the girl with the red hair was someone she'd seen in pictures at home—the wedding photo her father had kept on the mantel, the framed portrait that she'd had next to her bed and the family pictures that her grandparents had pasted in albums.

A rap at the window startled Nan out of her contemplation and she looked up to find Riley smiling at her. She quickly shoved the photo into her jacket pocket and hurried to the door. When he stepped inside, Nan wasn't quite sure what to do. She wanted to put the photo back where she'd found it, yet she needed time to examine it more closely.

She'd put it back later. No one would miss it, not with all the other photos tacked to the wall. Riley appeared in the doorway and Nan smiled. Her first impulse was to throw her arms around his neck and kiss him. But the ease they shared yesterday had been tempered by a night apart. "Hi," she said.

"Well, what kind of sorry greeting is that?" To her relief, Riley grabbed her around the waist and gave her a playful kiss. "Hello. You're up early. I expected you'd sleep the day away."

"No," she said, smiling up at him. "I feel great."

"You look great," he said, cupping her face with his hand. "Have you had breakfast yet?"

"Danny brought me coffee and some soda bread. I didn't have anything at the cottage to eat."

"Well, we'll have to go get you what you need. I'm just going to grab some coffee and we'll be off."

Nan retrieved her coffee from the pool table and gobbled down the rest of her bread, then wrapped the other two pieces in a bar napkin. When Riley returned with his coffee, he walked to the door and held it open. "Ireland awaits."

When they got outside, Nan remembered that the car was still at the cottage. "We'll have to walk back," she said. "I was afraid to bring the car."

"We can take my car," he said. He pointed to a Toyota SUV parked at the curb. The back hatch was open and Katie, the cook, was retrieving small crates and setting them on the sidewalk. "Thanks, darlin'."

"Your car? This is what you drive?"

"Yeah. I have to haul a lot of gear when I have a gig. And this morning, I hauled mussels from Bantry."

"If this car has an automatic transmission, I'm going to murder you," she said.

He chuckled as he opened her door. "Sorry. It's got

a gearshift. And no, I'm not going to let you drive this one until you've mastered the clown car."

"I've decided that I'm not going to learn how to drive that car. I'm just going to have you chauffeur me everywhere I want to go."

He closed her door, then got in the driver's side. "I think that's a grand plan. And where would you like to go this morning?"

"I need to buy some groceries."

They took off out of town, the morning breeze blowing through the sunroof of Riley's SUV. As they drove up into the hills, the roads grew more winding and the landscape more rugged. "Why are there no trees?" she asked. "I expected forests."

"Ah, that's a long and complicated story," he said.

"Tell me," Nan said. "I want to know."

"Ireland is a great rock of an island. Many years ago, the land was covered with trees, but people started to clear the higher land for pastures, mostly because there weren't as many trees up high to clear. But without the trees, the good soil washed down to the lowlands and the only thing that would grow up high was heather. The heather doesn't decompose and the new just keeps growing on top of the old and it makes peat. Peat soaks up water and turns land into a bog. And trees won't grow in a bog." He shrugged. "And pretty soon, all the trees were gone, high and low, cut for fuel or furniture."

"I still think it's beautiful," she said. "Just the way it is. It's wild and natural. Kind of uncivilized."

"Did you bring your camera?" he asked. "We'll stop at Healy Pass. There's a grand overlook there that I think you'd like. Though the Cahas aren't the Alps, they're the highest in Cork."

She reached in her pocket and pulled out her camera, but the photo fell out onto the console between them. Nan quickly picked it up, but not before Riley saw it.

"What's that?"

She held it out to him, hoping he'd forgive her for taking it from the pub. "It's a photo of my mother," Nan replied, holding it out to him. "I found it at the pub. I didn't mean to take it, but I wanted to look at it more closely."

"I'm sure it won't be missed," he said. "Those photos were in the pub when my folks bought it, so I can't tell you much about them." He stared at it. "Which one is she?"

"The one in the middle with the red hair," she said. "At least I think that's her."

"Pretty," he commented. He handed it back to Nan. "It's easy to see where you got your fine looks."

Nan frowned. "I don't think I look like her at all. I think I resemble my dad. He had dark hair when he was young."

They drove on, Nan staring at the photo and ignoring the landscape. All of the people in the photo had known her mother. And some of those people might have lived in Ballykirk. She flipped the photo over, hoping there might be an inscription on the back identifying the subjects, but it was blank.

If any of the people were from the village, someone would have to recognize them. And that might lead her to another person who might have known her mother.

Nan ran her fingers over the photo. They all looked so young and happy. Her mother's smile was so bright, her face alive with happiness.

As they continued their drive, Nan thought about her reasons for coming to Ireland. Was she chasing a ghost? The last two years of Laura Galvin's life were spent in and out of hospitals and before that, Nan had only scant recollections of the lively and laughing woman.

All she knew was that there was an empty spot inside of her, as if part of her identity was missing. She wasn't sure who to be or how to be. And when it came to love, she had nothing but romantic movies and books to guide her.

How many times had she wondered about love, about all the things that a mother told her daughter on the subject? No one had ever explained how it was supposed to feel. She'd never really seen it at home. Of all the questions she'd dreamed about asking her mother, that had been the most important. How would she know when she met the right man? How would it feel?

"Here we are," Riley said. He turned onto the edge of the road. "We'll have to walk a bit, but it will be worth it."

Nan looked out the window, surprised by the change in the landscape and the weather. The powerful rugged beauty of the land took her breath away and she stared at the unearthly sight, made even more strange by the wispy fog that hung over it all. Everywhere she looked was a picture waiting to be snapped, a perfect postcard image of a countryside so stunning it made her heartache.

Nan tucked the photo back into her pocket as she jumped out of the truck. From where she stood, she could look out at the valley below and the winding road that cut through it. Behind her, the mountains rose higher, huge craggy slabs of stone jutting into the gloomy sky.

"If we hike up a ways, there's a better view," Riley said. He took her hand and laced his fingers through hers. A flood of warmth rushed through her at his touch. Yesterday, she'd been all alone in the world. And today, she had this man who wanted to spend time with her, a man who enjoyed kissing and touching her. A man who wanted to spend the night in her bed.

Nan leaned into his body and smiled. As she came around the truck, she noticed two sheep observing them from across the road. They jumped off the small ledge they were standing on and headed toward her.

A tiny scream slipped from her throat and she held tight to Riley's arm as they nudged her, sticking their noses beneath her jacket.

"Get off, you tossers!" he said, pushing the sheep aside. "The tourists feed them and now they stand around waiting for something tastier than turf."

Nan laughed as one of the sheep butted her in the backside. She ran up the road and the determined sheep trotted after her. "I love Ireland," she called to Riley, throwing her arms out to the sky.

THEY HIKED UP to the top of the pass, stopping at the solitary house on the road, now turned into a shop that sold souvenirs and ice cream. Riley bought a cone and they shared it as they continued on up to the grotto.

The four white statues depicting Mary at the cross were set into the mountainside, a stark contrast to the gray surrounding them. Though he wasn't a particularly religious man, after a lifetime spent in a land filled with Catholic monuments, he'd come to appreciate how much a part of him it all was.

"Are you Catholic?" he asked.

She shook her head. "My mother was before she was married. My mother's parents were. But I was baptized Episcopalian."

Slowly, he was learning things about her, tiny facts that really didn't change his feelings for her, but completed the picture. "We have a thing for the Virgin Mary here in Ireland."

"It's beautiful," she said.

They continued on up the pass, to its highest point. Though he drove through the pass almost weekly, he'd never stopped to really look at it through a stranger's eyes. "They named this spot one of the top ten most romantic places in Ireland," he said.

"Is that why you brought me here?" Nan asked.

"I'd forgotten about it until now," he said. "When we read the news article at the pub we were all laughing. How could they have called this pile of rocks romantic? But I see it now. I guess it all has to do with the person you're with."

When they got to the top of the rise, they stood alone at the overlook. "We've one foot in County Cork and one foot in County Kerry," he said. Riley pointed toward the view. "There is the River Kenmare and Glen-more Lake. And just through those mountains, you can see Bantry Bay, not far from Ballykirk."

"It is romantic," she said, wrapping her arms around his waist. "But it would be more romantic if you kissed me."

"Are you giving me orders now, woman?" he teased. "I can't just be kissing you whenever the mood strikes."

"Well, you don't have to do anything. I'll do all the work."

"Make it good," Riley warned. He closed his eyes and puckered his mouth. Nan started laughing and he looked at her, glad to see that he could tease her out of a quiet mood.

"Stop," she said, grabbing his chin. "Make your mouth go the right way."

"Like this?" He pulled another face and she patted his lips with her fingers. "How about this?"

"No. Just make your mouth soft. Now, part your lips just a little bit." She smiled. "There. That's better."

"Are you ready now? Or maybe you'd like me to stand on my head?"

"I'm ready." As she moved closer, they both kept their eyes open and at the last moment, a fit of giggles overtook her. "This is not going to work. I can't kiss you if you're acting silly."

He softly touched his lips to hers. "Yes, you can. You can't resist me."

"I do like you," Nan said. "You're a very likeable guy."

"A sound bloke," he said.

"A straight-up dude," she said, putting on a slacker voice.

He smoothed his hand through her hair. "So we're all right? You seemed…preoccupied earlier in the car."

"I was. But it wasn't about you."

"You were thinking about your ma." He gave her a fierce hug. "Don't be sad about that. You'll find her here. At least what she left behind. You have the letters and now the photo. Who knows what other clues we'll find?"

She pulled the photo from her pocket. "Do you recognize anyone in the picture?"

"How would I—" He examined the photo more intently. "It was taken in front of the pub, I can tell you that. See there? That's what the shutters used to look like before my da made new ones." His brow furrowed. "I don't know. No one looks even vaguely familiar. But this was taken when? When I was a year old? My da might know. Or Jimmy McPhee, his old partner. He still lives in Ballykirk. He owned the pub when this photo was taken, before my da came in as a partner. He's about eighty now, but his mind is still sharp."

"Would you ask him?"

"We'll both go," he said. "We can stop by on our way back to the cottage."

"I'm almost afraid to know for sure," Nan said. "If he tells me that red-haired woman is Molly Malone from Dublin, I'll probably start crying and I'll make a fool out of myself."

"Don't worry. I've got a perfectly good sleeve here to wipe your tears away."

She smiled at him, then pulled out her camera and turned it on. Wrapping her arm around his neck, she pressed a kiss to his cheek and snapped a picture. When it came up on the screen, she showed it to him. "You and me in the most romantic place in Ireland," she said.

He pulled her into a playful embrace and nuzzled her neck. "Oh, I think we can do much better than that!"

WHEN NAN HAD BOOKED her trip to Ireland, she'd sketched out an entire itinerary, each day planned down to the hour. But now, she realized that all she wanted to do was to let the next nine days unfold in front of her, full of surprises.

Shopping for groceries had been an exercise in silliness, with Riley providing commentary on everything she put in her trolley, as he called it. She'd purchased enough food to last her for a week and mentally planned out a meal for that evening, hoping that Riley would agree to stay for supper if an invitation were offered.

Though they'd both avoided the subject of what hadn't happened the night before, Nan had no doubt they'd be faced with the same choice tonight. Over the course of the day, she'd only confirmed the undeniable attraction between them. At every opportunity, Riley found an excuse to pull her into a kiss or to rest his hand at the small of her back or to run his fingers through her hair.

Though it hadn't gone further than mild displays of public affection, Nan felt the need growing between them. She saw the desire in his eyes, felt it in the way he held her. His desire was like the waves crashing against the rocks, slowly washing away her inhibitions, threatening to sweep her out to sea.

It was already impossible to control her feelings for him. With every hour that passed, she became more infatuated with him. No amount of self-censure seemed to help. Yes, she knew all the risks, but here, in this strange land, her usual common sense had inexplicably abandoned her.

When they reached the cottage, Riley helped her carry the groceries inside. Nan sorted them, putting some in the small refrigerator and others in the cabinets above the stove. But when she was finished, she realized that she'd neglected to buy anything decent to drink.

"Wine," she murmured. "I forgot to buy wine. And beer."

"Don't worry yourself. I'll bring some up from the pub."

"When you come for dinner tonight?" she asked.

"You're going to be cooking for me now?" Riley grinned.

"Yes. It's the least I can do after you drove me to the supermarket. Can you come or do you have to work?"

"I wouldn't miss it," he said. "But there is one thing I need to know."

"What's that?"

"Should I bring a toothbrush?"

Nan felt her cheeks warm and she pressed her face into his chest. Undeterred, Riley hooked his thumb beneath her chin and forced her gaze to meet his. "Am I being too bold then?"

"No," Nan murmured. "And it might be a good idea to bring other…necessities?" He smoothed his hands over her hips and pulled her against him, the action provocative. A shiver of anticipation skittered up her spine.

"That I can do," he said, leaning to whisper in her ear. "I'm thinking about kissing you again, and about carrying you into the bedroom and letting you have your way with me. But I think we should leave that until tonight, no?"

"Yes," she said breathlessly.

"So, we have two options. I can leave you and return tonight. Or, we could take ourselves down to Jimmy McPhee's place and have a chat."

"I vote for Jimmy McPhee's," she said.

"All right then, let's go."

They arrived at a small whitewashed cottage just minutes later, Riley pulling the SUV up to the front gate. "Jimmy is a notorious flirt," he warned. "He'll probably ask if he can kiss you and he's sure to grab your arse, so keep a watch out."

"You said he was eighty."

"Oh, that doesn't stop him. He may have slowed down a bit, but whenever he stops by the pub, he has the ladies buying him drinks all night long."

They knocked on the door and a few seconds later, it swung open to reveal an elderly man with pure white hair and twinkling blue eyes. His eyes widened when he caught site of Nan and he grabbed her hand. "Oh, Lord, my prayers have been answered. I'll forget about winnin' the lottery if you'll just let me keep the girl."

"Afternoon, Jimmy," Riley said, snatching Nan's hand from the old man. "We've come to see you to ask a question. Can we come in for a chat?"

"Only if you'll stay for a cup o' tea," he said, stepping back to allow them inside. "Come, come. And mind your manners, Riley Quinn. Introduce me to your lovely friend."

"This is Nan Galvin. She's come all the way to Ballykirk from America."

"America? I have a cousin in America. He lives in Boston. You wouldn't happen to know him, would you? His name is Bobby McPhee."

She glanced over at Riley. "I'm afraid not. I live a long way from Boston. In Wisconsin."

"Sit," he said. "I just put a pot on. I'll be right back."

She and Riley took a spot on the sofa. Riley took her hand and gave it a squeeze. Nan reached into her pocket and pulled out the photo and looked down at it. What were the odds he'd remember a girl from twenty-seven summers ago? Yes, her mother had been an American, so she might have stood out as different. But after so many years?

When Jimmy returned, he poured them all a cup of tea, then passed around a plate of cookies. Nan was too nervous to drink or eat and as soon as he settled himself in a comfortable chair, she held the photo out to him.

"I was hoping you'd remember the people in this snapshot," she said. "It was taped up on the wall of the pub. It was taken about twenty-seven years ago."

He took the picture and studied it for a long time,

then pulled his glasses out of his shirt pocket and put them on.

"They would have been in their early twenties," Nan continued.

"This would have been about 1984," Riley added. "About eight years before my da bought in to the pub."

Jimmy cocked his head to the side, as if he were trying to retrieve a memory from deep in his mind. He pointed to the photo, tapping at it. "One of these boys looks familiar. What was his name? Oh, he was a chancer, that one. He lived out on that farm the other side of Trafask, just around the big bend on the Glengarriff Road."

"Where the Donnelys live? The place with the pond?"

"That's it," he said. "He used to work one of the fishing boats out of Ballykirk. Now what was his—ah, there it is. Tiernan. His name was Tiernan Findley."

Nan sucked in a sharp breath. "You're sure? Tiernan?"

"Sure I am. And his da was Carey."

Her pulse quickened and she had to remind herself to breathe. What did this mean? Had her mother named her after this boy? And why would she have done that?

"I remember him and his da hanging about the pub. He was there one summer and then he was gone. I remember something of a drowning."

"Do they still live on the farm?" Riley asked.

Jimmy shook his head. "As I recall, his da sold the farm maybe fifteen years ago. Don't know where he went. But you could ask Kenny Craig. He leased his land before Findley sold."

Nan's mind was spinning, wondering what this boy named Tiernan had meant to her mother. Were they just friends? Or had they been more? And why would she have chosen to name her only child after a boy she met in a pub in Ballykirk, Ireland? A horrible thought occurred to her. What if Tiernan had died in the accident and she'd been named in his memory?

The possibilities began to overwhelm her and she felt the room closing in on her. She quickly stood. "I—I have to go," she murmured. "It was a pleasure meeting you, but I have to go." She stumbled over Riley's feet as she squeezed past him and headed for the door.

"I'll be going, too, Jimmy. But thanks."

"Is the lass all right?" Jimmy asked.

"I think all this talk of her departed mother might be a bit upsetting."

By the time she got to the front door, Riley was behind her, his hands firm on her waist. She hurried outside, drawing deep breaths of the fresh afternoon air. "He's dead. I know it. My mother named me after that boy because he died. He was her friend and he died. And maybe she loved him."

"You don't know that. We don't have all the answers yet."

He drew her toward his car, but Nan stopped short. "I think I'm going to walk home," she said. "I just want to let this settle for a while."

"All right," Riley said. "Are we still on for tonight?"

She nodded. "Yes. Of course. I'll see you at seven?"

"Sounds grand," he said. He walked with her out the gate, then kissed her cheek. "Don't drive yourself mad over this, Nan. We don't know anything for certain yet. Worry about it when you know for sure."

He obviously didn't know anything about her, Nan thought to herself. She had always been an expert at turning molehills into mountains. She nodded and started off down the road in the opposite direction.

When she turned back, she saw Riley watching her from beside his car, a look of concern etched on his handsome features. He was right. Wasting energy wondering about things that might not be was silly. Maybe Tiernan was happy and healthy and he'd be able to tell her all about her mother. She'd put her worries aside for now and think about them later.

She gave him a wave and he returned it. Maybe it was fate that she'd rented his cottage. Maybe she was destined to meet him so that he'd be able to help her with her search. But was that all it was supposed to be? Or were they meant to be more to each other?

So many questions. But was she really ready to know all the answers?

4

"Well, aren't you a Dicky Dazzler."

Riley gave his older brother, Kellan, a pointed glare, then turned to Danny, who stood behind the bar at the pub. "Go find me a good bottle or two of wine," he said. "Not the cheap stuff. And bring up three or four bottles of that Belgian ale."

"Red or white, yer royal bog-trotter?" Danny asked.

Kellan slapped his younger brother's hand. "Good one, Danny. Clever and cutting all at once."

"Funny," Riley muttered. "And give me a whiskey while I wait."

His brother poured him two fingers and slid the glass across the bar. "So what's the special occasion? You're wearing a shirt that's been pressed and a jacket you only take out at Christmas. And why is it you always dress like a culchie but you have more money than God?"

Though Kellan made a fine living as an architect and Danny did well as an artisan blacksmith and metal sculptor, Riley had been the most fortunate financially. The royalties from his CDs brought in a third of his annual income and performing made up the other two-thirds.

Still, both Danny and Kellan had a solid future in front of them. The one thing about fame was that it could be fleeting. Riley never knew when the crowds would move on to someone else, when the offers of work would dry up and he'd become just another washed-up pub singer who'd made a few decent CDs.

It had never really bothered him until now. Riley had always put off the worry until it actually came about. But now, thoughts of his future had been pushed into his head and he couldn't seem to rid himself of them. Was it Nan who had brought on the confusion?

It was far too early to think about a future with her. And who said he couldn't find more profitable and dependable work if he needed to? He could write pop songs or produce other singers. Or he could go to university and study something completely unrelated to music. He was a clever lad. He had plenty of options.

"Well, are you going to tell us, or are you planning to spend the night staring into your glass of whiskey?" Kellan asked.

"I have a date. A dinner date."

"With the American?" Kellan asked. "When do I get a look at this girl?"

"Oh, she's grand," Danny assured him. "Though why she's wasting her time with Riley is a question that's been plaguing my mind. It's keeping me up at night."

Kellan arched his brow. "That so? Well, at least something is keeping you up at night because it sure isn't a woman."

"I like her," Riley said. "I'll admit it. And I haven't a clue why. She's pretty enough, but she's not like any other girl I've dated. She's just really…sweet."

"I've heard American girls are wild as banshees in the bedroom," Danny said. "What say you, Riley? Is it true?"

"I've known her for a day and a half," he said. "We haven't had the pleasure yet. Not that I'd be telling you if we had."

Kellan shook his head. "You're movin' too slow, brother." His smile faded. "She'll go home. They all go home. That's the advantage of snogging a tourist. But don't let yourself fall too hard, boyo. It's not worth it."

"Yeah, yeah," Riley said. He gulped down his whiskey. "I know." Setting the glass down, he stared into it for a long moment. "I'm not sure I'm going to be able to stop myself on this one, though. It's feeling different than the rest."

"Why is that?" Kellan asked.

"I couldn't tell you," he said, shaking his head. "She's just going through some things now and I feel like I can at least help her out."

"You're going to rescue her," Danny said. "Just like Da rescued Ma. You know what that means, don't you?"

"Yes, I'll be getting my own wine and beer," Riley said, pushing away from the bar.

"Hey, you're still playing here Saturday night, right?"

"Yeah," Riley said. "The band and me have rehearsal that afternoon at three, so make sure you post that we're closed. We'll play at nine. Maggie Griffith called and said she'd open for us at seven."

"And what about Dublin?" Danny asked. "Aren't you supposed to be in the studio next week working on your new CD?"

"I don't need a feckin' social secretary, Danny. I know where I'm supposed to be and when."

"Just askin'," Danny said.

Riley cursed beneath his breath as he walked back into the kitchen and down the steps to the cellar. He pulled a bottle of red and one of white and put them in an old basket, then added six bottles of beer.

Yes, he was supposed to be in Dublin next week, recording vocals for the band's new CD. And he'd had every intention of going, until Nan showed up in town. Now, he was searching for excuses to make, anything to delay for another week. He settled on a sore throat, brought on by a wicked summer cold. It sounded plausible enough. And though studio time was tricky to schedule, the delay would be worth it.

Riley snuck out the back door of the kitchen, unwilling to suffer any more of his brothers' taunting. They were the ones to talk, he mused. Neither Kellan nor Danny had had a woman in their lives for months. Who was to say that they wouldn't turn their lives upside down for the right one?

As he walked, he passed his car by, choosing to hike the two kilometers up to the cottage. If he did spend the night with Nan, Riley didn't want to give the village gossips something to talk about for the rest of the week. Although, word had probably gotten out already, after the rather passionate and very public kiss they'd shared in the pub the night before.

Several cars passed by him on the road and honked their horns in greeting. Halfway up to the cottage, he ran into Fergus O'Malley and his six dogs. "Good evening to you, Riley Quinn," Fergus called.

"Evening, Fergus."

"Are you up to see your lady then?" he asked, pointing to the cottage.

Riley groaned inwardly. If Fergus O'Malley knew he and Nan were spending time together, then the gossip had spread much more quickly than he'd ever anticipated. "Just delivering some necessities," Riley said, holding up the crate.

Fergus chuckled. "Oh, is that what they call it nowadays? Deliverin' necessities." He continued to laugh as he walked past, the dogs trotting dutifully behind him.

Picking up his pace, Riley strode up the hill, determined to avoid any other meetings with curious townsfolk. When he reached the front door of the cottage, he took a moment to catch his breath, then rapped on the door. A few seconds later it opened, to a sight that made his heart skip a beat.

She looked more beautiful that he'd ever imagined her to be. A pale blue dress, cut deep in the front and made of some silky fabric, clung to her slender body. Her arms were exposed and her feet and legs were bare beneath the flowing skirt.

Riley glanced up at her face to find her regarding him quizzically. "Sorry," he said. "I was gawking. You look absolutely grand."

This observation brought a beautiful smile to her face. "Thank you. So do you."

"May I come in?" Riley asked.

She stepped aside. "You may. You do own the place."

The cottage was filled with lovely smells. He wasn't sure what it was she'd prepared, but Riley knew that even if it was inedible, he'd devour it with a smile. "I brought wine and beer," he said.

Nan reached for the basket. "I'll put the beer in the fridge."

"I'll do it. I know where it is."

The kitchen was tiny, with barely enough room for the sink, the cooker and the refrigerator, never mind two people. Nan watched as he put the bottles in the freezer to chill. "We're having spaghetti," she said. "I hope you like Italian food."

"I could eat," he said. But he didn't want to think about food. All he wanted at the moment was to pull her into his arms and kiss her. Riley followed her out of the kitchen and then, to his surprise, she turned around and threw herself into his arms, kissing him desperately.

With a low groan, Riley furrowed his fingers through her hair and her lips molded to his. A surge of desire washed through him, hot and liquid, a fire in his veins.

Kissing her wasn't enough. He wanted to be closer, his desire consuming her body as well. His hands skimmed over her curves, kneading the soft flesh beneath the fabric of her dress. He fought the urge to tear the garment from her body, impatient with the pace of a proper seduction.

But Nan didn't have the same concerns about the

speed they were moving. Her fingers fumbled with the buttons of his shirt and when they were all undone, she yanked his shirttail out of his jeans. In one deft motion, she shoved the jacket and shirt off his shoulders, never once breaking the kiss they shared.

Riley struggled with the buttons on the cuffs before he was able to rid himself of the clothes. His hands immediately returned to her body in an unchecked exploration. He bunched her skirt in his fists and when it was up around her thighs, slid his hands beneath to cup her backside.

Through it all, they moved inexorably toward the bedroom, a step at a time. Dinner had been forgotten, life had been forgotten. All Riley could think about was the feel of her body beneath his hands. Anticipation built inside of him and he wondered if he'd even be able to stop now that they'd begun.

When Nan began to work on the button on his jeans, he decided it was time to dispose of her dress. He reached down and grabbed the hem, then pulled it off over her head, leaving her in just her lacy underwear.

Everywhere he touched was a new experience, each delicious curve and limb a revelation. Riley had always loved the female body and its ability to spark his desire, but there had never been such a deep need before. Though they'd only known each other two days, he was keenly aware of the connection growing between them.

When she'd finished with the zipper of his jeans, he kicked off his shoes. Without a pause, Nan slipped her palms beneath the waistband and skimmed the faded denim down over his hips. Finally, she broke the desperate kiss between them and smiled up at him.

"Better?" he asked, unable to keep from grinning himself.

"Much better."

"If I'd have known this was appropriate dinner attire, I wouldn't have bothered getting dressed at all. I could have walked up here starkers."

"You'll have to try that next time," she teased. Nan ran her hand down his chest, letting a finger hook the elastic of his boxers. She gave it a snap. "We're all undressed and no place to go."

"Oh, I think I know where we can go," he said.

She laughed. "I'll race you." With that, she turned and ran toward the bedroom. It took him two quick steps to catch her around the waist. Riley picked her up off her feet and carried her into the bedroom, then tumbled onto the bed with her. Then he remembered the condoms he'd put in his jacket pocket.

"Bloody hell," he muttered. "I'll be right back."

"Where are you going?"

"For some necessities," he said. When he returned, she was stretched out on the bed, her elbows braced behind her. He held up the string of five condoms. "Wouldn't want to be without these," he said.

She arched her eyebrow. "Only five? Stingy boy."

"Cheeky bird," he countered. Riley jumped onto the bed and stretched out above her, pinning her hands on either side of her head.

He'd been hard since he'd pulled off her dress and

now, his shaft pressed against her hips, fully aroused and ready. Leaning in, he softly touched his mouth to hers, then tasted more deeply. Slowly, he thought to himself. They'd already raced through the first part of foreplay and he wanted the anticipation to last as long as possible.

But Nan had other ideas. She twisted beneath him as he kissed her, trying to free her hands and creating an irresistible friction between their bodies. He moaned as her hand finally slid beneath his boxers.

Riley wanted her fingers wrapped around him if only to experience the sensations her touch created. He grabbed her waist and rolled her on top of him, giving her complete freedom to do what she wanted.

"No more clothes," she whispered, reaching back to unhook her bra. Taking her cue, he tugged her panties down, but they got tangled between them. She stood up on the bed, then slowly drew them down, watching him with a teasing smile.

"You are very naughty," he said.

Nan pointed to his boxers. Chuckling, he pulled them off, then tossed them to her. "Better?"

She let her gaze slowly drift down the length of his body, then back again. "Yes. Much better." As she dropped back down, straddling his hips, Riley couldn't help but wonder if she were deliberately tormenting him. Everything she did seemed designed to push him closer and closer to the edge.

He spanned her waist with his hands, holding her still as she leaned down to kiss him again. She had the perfect body, made for his touch. Everything fit, everything worked. She shifted above him and he nearly slipped inside of her.

Groaning, Riley reached out for the condoms, but she took them out of his hand and tore one of the packages open. With deft fingers, she smoothed the latex over his shaft. And then, she was above him, wet and ready.

Riley wanted to slow down, but Nan would have none of it. Slowly, she took him inside her, inch by inch, until he was completely buried. A sigh slipped from her lips and she closed her eyes. Riley watched her and waited for her to move again, but she seemed content to revel in the quiet power of their joined bodies.

When she began to move, Riley groaned, drawing her into a long, deep kiss. But the taste of her mouth was not enough to distract from the feel of her body surrounding him. Nan seemed to follow her instincts, moving with him and then against him, as they both moved toward their release.

And then, she was there, tensing above him, her head thrown back, her eyes closed. Her body stiffened before she dissolved into soft shudders of pleasure. Riley held back, watching and waiting until she was nearly spent. He drove into her, holding tight to her hips.

His orgasm hit him like a bolt of lightning, electrifying every nerve in his body. One moment, he was rational and aware, and then the next, he was lost in an exquisite release. Wave after wave of pleasure coursed through him.

When it was over, he opened his eyes and found her looking down at him, a satisfied smile twitching at her lips. With a lazy groan, she stretched out on top of him, nuzzling her face into his chest. "Forget about dinner," she said. "I'm not even hungry anymore."

"Maybe if we just rest a bit we'll regain our appetite," he said.

"For sex or food?" she asked, looking up at him.

"Sex. And then maybe food."

"Or food and then sex," she suggested.

"So you're hungry?"

"Famished," she said.

"Then I think we'd better take care of that right away."

BETWEEN THE SEX and the food, Nan wasn't sure that there was anything else in the world she required at the moment. After an hour of lying in bed, recovering from their rather impetuous encounter, Riley decided he needed nourishment.

They laid out an erotic picnic in the middle of Nan's bed, the tangled sheets serving as their table linens. Nan prepared two bowls with the pasta and sauce and Riley opened the wine and filled two coffee mugs.

Sex had always been such a nerve-racking experience in the past. She'd always wondered if she was doing everything she was supposed to do, whether she was pleasing the man she was with. But with Riley, there were no questions. It all felt perfectly natural.

Was this normal? Nan wondered. Had those others simply been the wrong person at the wrong time? Or had her inhibitions held her back from really enjoying herself?

"This is really good," he said, twirling the spaghetti around his fork.

"It's not," she said. "I'm not much of a cook. Pasta is the limit of my gourmet skills. But if you add enough Parmesan cheese, anything tastes good."

"We don't serve pasta at the pub. We're meat-and-potatoes kind of guys."

"Meat and potatoes and more potatoes," she said.

"Yeah, well, if you can't decide what kind of potato you'd like with your meal, we give you three choices on the plate." He pointed to a basket near her foot. "Can I have more of that bread?"

"I was going to make garlic bread, but I thought it best to leave off the garlic." She sent him a coy smile. "I thought we might be doing some kissing."

"And heavy breathing," he said.

Riley set his bowl down and reached out to grab her foot, gently massaging it. "I thought this was going to happen, but I didn't think it would be quite so...intense."

Nan breathed a silent sigh of relief. He'd been pleased. The five lovers she'd had in her life hadn't been particularly adventuresome when it came to sex. But she'd decided before Riley arrived that she wasn't going to let anything that happened in the past get in the way of what she wanted with him.

Now that their first time was over, she felt like a different woman. With Riley, she was free to explore her desires. He didn't know her well enough to judge her or to question her experience.

"It was good," she said, unable to suppress a smile.

He kissed the arch of her foot. "I love to see you smile."

"I'm happy," she said. "I'm having a very good vacation."

"We haven't talked about your snapshot. Did you decide what you wanted to do?"

"I haven't thought about it," she said. "I came here looking for my mother, but I think I'm finding myself instead."

He met her gaze with a serious expression. "Really?"

"So much of who we become as adults has to do with our parents. I don't remember much of my mother so sometimes I feel like I don't really know how to be a woman. I know it doesn't make sense because I am a woman. But there are pieces missing. And I'm not sure what they are."

"I don't understand," he said.

Nan looked at him for a long moment, her brow furrowed, wondering if she was ready to reveal something so intimate. "Sex, for one. I've had lovers, but I never really felt anything. I knew how it worked, but it didn't really make sense. Until now."

"And what did you feel?"

"Free," she said. "Completely free. I didn't have to think, I just felt. And it was perfect. I know it sounds silly, but it's important. And a bit unexpected."

"I'm glad I could be of service," he said, a teasing smile curling the corners of his mouth. He leaned over and kissed her breast. "Is there anything else I can help you with?"

"I'm not sure."

"Well, I am. Sure, that is. I'm absolutely certain that I want to spend the next eight days and nights in this cottage with you."

"Don't you have to work?"

"My brothers and cousin will cover the shifts at the pub. I have to sing on Saturday night, but you can come along for that. I'm completely yours. So, what should we do for your third day in Ireland? And please note, that spending the day in bed would be my number-one choice."

"I think we should plan to sleep in tomorrow morning," she said. "And then we should find a wonderful place for lunch and see something interesting."

"We have food in the refrigerator and I think your body is very interesting."

"I'm not spending the whole day in bed," she said. "I'm supposed to go see things and do things. I have it all planned out."

"And what were you supposed to be doing tonight?"

"A stroll through Ballykirk, exploring the harbor and then dinner at a picturesque Irish pub."

"Yet, this is so much better," he said. "Naked Italian picnic followed by incredible sex with a handsome Irish bloke."

"I didn't come here for sex," Nan said. In truth, she'd expected her vacation to be interesting and illuminating. But this had completely exceeded expectations.

He handed her his mug. "All right, then we'll stop doing this. Full stop. Right now." He crawled out of bed and began to gather their clothes. "We'd best get dressed or the temptation might become too much to deny."

"No," Nan protested. "Come back to bed."

With a satisfied smile, he flopped back down on the bed and continued to massage her foot. "Well, I'm glad we've gotten that out of the way, aren't you?"

"You think you're all that, don't you," Nan teased. "Why do I get the feeling you've always had your way with girls and I'm just another name on the list?"

His expression clouded over and he sat up and grabbed his empty bowl and his mug of wine, placing them on the floor beside the bed. Bracing his hands on either side of her body, he leaned forward, his lips just inches from hers.

"You are unlike any other woman I've known, Nan Galvin," he said. "And if you think I'm taking this lightly, you're quite mistaken."

A tremor raced through her. His words were so direct, so heartfelt, that Nan had no choice but to believe them. And yet, she knew Riley was an accomplished flirt. Men like him could make a woman believe anything.

"And what will you do when I leave?" she murmured.

"You haven't left yet. And I expect I'll deal with that when you do." Riley held out his hand. "Give me that bowl. And your mug."

"Why?" she asked, holding the bowl just out of his reach. "I'm not sharing. I'm still hungry."

"Trust me. This will be better than pasta."

She handed him the bowl and mug and he set it on the bedside table. Then, he reached out and pulled her naked body beneath his, their limbs tangling in the sheets. "Time for dessert," he said with a low growl.

He kissed her, a long, lingering kiss meant to provoke her passion.

"This is supposed to be better than my pasta?" she laughed. "Oh, please. I've had stale brownies out of a vending machine that were tastier."

"You eat brownies?" He frowned. "How does one—"

"Not brownies, like elves," she explained. "Brownies are little squares of chocolate cake, only better than cake."

"That makes more sense," he said, cupping her breast with his palm. He teased the nipple, rubbing his thumb over the hard peak. "There's this."

"Still not as good as the stale brownie. But slightly better than two-month-old ice cream."

He replaced his thumb with his tongue, sucking gently until Nan giggled. "Oh, now that's better. Now we're talking about caramel corn—without peanuts."

"What is this obsession that Americans have with peanuts?" he asked, slowly kissing his way down her belly. When he found the crease between her legs, he slowly teased at it with his tongue.

"Oh, that's quite lovely," she said, arching back on the bed, clutching at the sheets. "Tiramisu."

He teased until she spread her legs, giving him complete control of her body. She found it amazing how uninhibited she became when she was with Riley. In all her prior relationships, she'd been afraid to expose the depth of her need, thinking she might push the boundaries of propriety.

But Riley had taught her that when it came to sex,

at least with an Irishman, there were no rules. And enjoying herself was a requirement, not just a possibility.

Nan was quick to reach the edge, but Riley had already learned to read the signs of her impending orgasm. He carefully brought her close again and again and each time, she felt her frustration growing. But it wasn't impatience holding her back. She wanted to know how far outside herself he could take her, how it would feel to completely and utterly surrender to him.

She tangled her fingers in his hair, whispering his name, waves of sensation racing through her body. But Riley took his time, as if he wanted to prove to her that he could give her something no other man could. She would remember him and their time together, not just for the places they saw and the people they met, but for this.

Again and again, she hurdled toward the edge, only to have him gently draw her back again. But then, when she thought she might never find release, he let her go. The sheer exhilaration was enough to leave her gasping for breath and she felt herself falling and falling. The impact hit suddenly, her body exploding into long, intense spasms of pleasure.

Nan couldn't think, and for a moment, she lost touch with everything around her, focusing on the contact of his tongue as he continued to torment her. Finally, she pushed him away, unable to take any more, her body trembling and her nerves electrified.

He slowly kissed his way up her body, then curled against her, his head resting on her arm. "You'll never eat a stale brownie again without thinking of me," he murmured.

Nan laughed, then turned on her side and playfully slapped his chest. "It won't be just brownies. Every time I eat dessert, I'll think of you. Crème brûlée. Lemon meringue pie. Three-layer chocolate cake with mocha buttercream icing. And memories of Riley Quinn."

They lay in bed for a long time, talking and laughing. And then they made love again, this time slowly and deliberately, until they were both completely spent. And as Nan drifted off to sleep, she wondered if the next time she crawled into her bed at home, she would be wishing that Riley was right there with her.

MOONLIGHT POURED through the window of the bedroom, throwing a shaft of light onto the old quilt. They'd turned off the lamp hours ago and Riley had been left to look at her with only the faintest illumination.

She lay beside him, stretched out on her side, the sheet twisted around her waist, offering a tempting view of her naked body. He'd already memorized every beautiful feature of her face, every intriguing detail of her form, and yet he still wanted to just sit and stare.

He'd expected to fall into a deep sleep after another two hours of sex. But the exhaustion he usually felt had been replaced with a strange restlessness. He was energized, his thoughts more focused than at anytime during the day.

His mind whirled with ideas for lyrics and he pushed them aside, determined to fall asleep. Yet everything he'd felt and experienced that night had turned itself into music in his head. It had been so long since he experienced a burst like this and he'd wondered if his passion for songwriting had waned.

But now it was back, full force, and he felt the need to express himself, to pour everything onto the page before it was lost. Riley sat up in bed and ran his fingers through his messy hair.

He was twenty-eight and fast approaching thirty. Most singer-songwriters had made a name for themselves at this point. And if they hadn't, they'd made plans for the rest of their life. But thoughts of Nan had also brought thoughts of marriage and a family. Someday, he'd want that, but the life of a musician made family life doubly difficult.

His parents had offered to sell him the pub. None of his siblings wanted to run the Hound and Riley seemed like the logical choice since it would give him a permanent venue for his music. But it would also tie him to Ballykirk.

He'd always wanted the life of an itinerant Irish singer. It had always been enough, until now. But was it enough to convince a woman to cast her lot with him? He reached out and smoothed his hand over Nan's bare arm. She stirred, then slipped back into a deep sleep. Meeting Nan had taught him one thing: someday, there would be a woman he wanted to spend his life with. And he needed to be ready to offer her a future.

Riley sighed. He wanted to wake her, to continue their conversations, to learn everything he could about her. Was she the one he'd been waiting for? How would he know given their limited time together? And what if he let Nan leave, only to find that she had been the perfect woman for him?

Riley carefully rolled out of bed and pulled on his jeans. He walked, barefoot, to the front door, then slipped outside.

The wind off the sea buffeted his body and whipped at his hair. He closed his eyes and took a deep breath, trying to clear his head. A melody drifted through his head and suddenly, there were words to go with it. He slowly walked down the garden path to the gate, then back again.

It was a good idea, something he ought to write down before he forgot it. Wasn't this a laugh, he thought to himself. He hadn't written a decent tune in months and now, a night of good sex had turned that all around. Hell, if he continued on with Nan, he might have a whole new album by the end of the week.

When he got back inside, he searched through the top drawer in a chest, pulling out a small pad of paper and a pen. He flipped on a lamp near the sofa and sat down, determined to write all his ideas out and then put the pad away and go back to bed.

But an hour later, when the clock on the mantel struck four, Riley realized that he was glad he hadn't been able to sleep. Lyrics had poured onto the page, line after line, and each with a melody to go with it. When the lyrics were complete, he went back and added harmonies, sketching out the guitar chords above the words.

He thought about putting on a pot of coffee, but decided to keep working until exhaustion set in naturally.

Instead, he got up and fetched a beer from the refrigerator, twisting the cap off as he walked back to the sofa. He spread the three songs out on the floor in front of him, studying them for a long time.

They were good. Really, really good. And they needed to go on the new CD. He had his reason to delay recording. Who knew what he'd come up with in the next week? And the band would have to have time to practice these.

"What are you doing out here?"

The sound of her voice startled him and he glanced over his shoulder to find Nan standing in the bedroom door, her naked body wrapped in the quilt from the bed. "Hey," he said. "I'm sorry. I just couldn't sleep."

She walked over to him and plopped down beside him on the sofa. "Are you writing?"

He nodded. "Yeah. I'm not sure where the inspiration came from but—no, that's not true. I think I know where the inspiration came from."

"Where?"

"From what went on in that bedroom," he said. "I just felt this need to write about it."

"About sex?"

"No, just about men and women. Passion. Love. All of those things that singers sing about."

She pulled her feet up on the sofa and snuggled up against him. "Sing me one of them," she murmured, closing her eyes.

"They're not ready yet," he said, turning to drop a kiss on the top of her head. Riley sat back, resting his cheek on her soft hair. "But when they're ready, you'll be the first one I sing them to."

"Mmm," she said. "That's nice. I like your voice."

She nestled closer and a few minutes later, her breathing slowed and she fell asleep. Riley reached for the notepad and pen, then let his mind wander again. He'd never believed in the concept of an artistic muse. But maybe that's what Nan was for him—a source of inspiration in human form.

Riley ran his hand over her silken hair and down her arm. He'd spent a lot of his life searching, looking for that one thing that would guarantee him complete happiness. And as he sat in this simple cottage, with Nan beside him, Riley couldn't think of anything else in the world he wanted.

Right now, for this single moment in time, he was completely and utterly happy. And if he could stop time in its place, he would. But Riley couldn't forget that Nan would be leaving him. When that time came, he wondered if he'd ever experience such pure contentment again.

5

NAN SMELLED the coffee before she opened her eyes. She sighed softly and buried her face in the down pillow, stretching her arms above her head. This was becoming a habit after three nights together. Riley was up at the crack of dawn, scribbling things in his notebook and strumming on his guitar, and she slept until at least nine or ten.

Yesterday, they'd taken a drive to the Burren, a vast stone plateau in County Clare. Though the landscape was stark and harsh, it was still beautiful. Mounds of colorful wildflowers punctuated the gray slabs of stone and everywhere she looked, there were birds and small animals to watch.

They'd had a pub lunch in Ennis, then stopped in every village along their route to Lough Learie. A drive around the lake was followed by a gourmet dinner in Killarney and a long ride home.

Yesterday had been the first day she'd followed her carefully planned itinerary. And though she'd seen everything on her plan, it had been marred by the sight of the signs for Shannon Airport. She hadn't wanted to think about going home, but there was no ignoring it as they drove through Limerick.

Though she'd tried to limit the depth of her affection for Riley, the attempt had been a pitiful failure. With every minute that she spent in his presence, she grew more attached, more certain that he was the man she was meant to find.

It had all been such a whirlwind, her feelings coming so quickly. And she'd tried to tell herself that this somehow diminished the truth in what she felt. It wasn't love, but merely an infatuation. And yet, every instinct told her the opposite. She was falling in love with Riley and she could do nothing to stop herself.

There had been so many moments when the words had come to her lips, when she'd nearly blurted them out. How would he react if he knew her true feelings? Was this still a holiday romance to him, an affair that would come to an end when she got on the plane to go home? Or was he feeling something deeper? She groaned softly. Though the physical part came so easily between them, the emotional part was messy and complicated.

"I know you want this," Riley whispered in a sing-song voice.

Her eyes still closed, she reached out for the mug but found only empty air. "Are you withholding my coffee for sex? You are a desperate man, Riley Quinn."

"I'm a happy man," he countered, sitting down on the edge of the bed.

She pushed up, bracing her hands beneath her and

opening her eyes. He'd already showered, his dark hair falling in damp strands over his forehead. All he wore was a pair of jeans, zipped but not buttoned at the waist. "Morning," she murmured.

"God, you are pretty in the morning. Your hair is sticking up in little spikes. And your eyes are all sleepy."

Nan reached up and combed her hair with her fingers. She knew exactly how she looked in the morning and she certainly wouldn't describe it as cute. "Are you going to give me that coffee? Or would you like me to smother you with this pillow?"

He held out the mug. "I walked down to the pub and brought up some soda bread and a fruit salad that Katie made. And orange juice."

"You brought me breakfast?" Nan smiled. "Come here. That deserves a kiss."

He leaned over and collected his reward, lingering as his tongue touched hers. It was the perfect way to wake up, quietly and romantically, not jarred to consciousness by an obnoxious alarm clock. "What time is it?"

"Just after ten," he said. "Early."

"I could spend my entire vacation in this bedroom," she said.

"I thought you liked running around like a mad woman."

"I'm sorry," she said. "I spent months mapping out everything I wanted to see. I got all the guidebooks and made lists and researched everything. And now—" She giggled. "I don't give a feck!"

"Bravo," Riley said. "I also have some news for you.

I did a little more detective work and I found out where Carey Findley lives. You remember, Tiernan Findley's father."

Nan sat up. She'd been so caught up with Riley that she'd pushed her search aside. A twinge of guilt twisted at her heart. Was it that easy to forget everything that brought her to Ireland?

"Carey Findley lives about thirty kilometers from here in a town called Kealkill. I put in a call but he wasn't home, so I left a message."

"What did you say? Did you tell him about me?"

"I just asked him to contact me at the pub. That's all. Now we just have to wait for him to call."

Nan wrapped her arms around her knees and stared down at her toes. "All right. I guess that's good. When he calls, we'll go visit him and then we can talk about the letters he wrote to my mother. How long do you think it will be before he calls back?"

"We'll give him a day or two and if he doesn't call, we can take a drive over to his place and visit." Riley reached out and smoothed his hand over her cheek. "So, what are we doing today?"

"Your choice," she said. "Take me somewhere interesting. Show me something wonderful. Somewhere Irish and historical. Can we go kiss the Blarney stone?"

"No," Riley said. "Absolutely not. There are so many better things to do than hang upside down from the top of a castle and kiss a stone that thousands of people have put their lips on. From here on out, your lips belong exclusively to me."

"Yeah, kissing the stone doesn't sound very appealing." She took another sip of her coffee. "What have you been doing with yourself since you got up?"

"I've been working on a song I want to sing tomorrow night."

"Sing it for me now."

He shook his head. "No. Not until I'm ready."

"Do you just sing at the Hound?"

"No. All over Ireland. A lot in Dublin. Sometimes with my band, sometimes alone. Every now and then, we sing in London. I've written some songs for other singers and they've been successful. One was just used in an Irish film."

"So you like what you do?"

He shrugged. "Sometimes. And sometimes I think I ought to quit singing and get on with my real life. Become an upstanding citizen with a respectable job that provides a better living."

"Why?" she asked softly. "If you're happy, money shouldn't make a difference. I'll never become a millionaire working in a library, but I love doing what I do."

"I was never sure I wanted all the stuff that goes with fame and fortune anyway. You have to spend so much time trying to hang on to it that you never get a chance to enjoy it."

"I wish I had a talent," Nan said. "My mother used to be a wonderful artist. I have some of the watercolors she did. And my father could play the piano by ear. But I can't do anything exceptional."

"You drive me wild in the bedroom," he said. "And everywhere else. That's exceptional."

"I suspect you have a lot of women willing to drive you wild," she said, reaching out and running her hand down his bare chest.

"Until you walked out of those doors at Shannon Airport, I'd been perfectly sane for many months." He grabbed her coffee and took a sip. "I've told you about my work, what about yours? You work in a library."

"I'm the assistant director of special collections," she said. "I work at a university library."

"What does that mean? What kind of collections? Comic books? Marbles?"

"I'm second in charge of rare books and maps and old letters and everything that's not a regular book and is old and valuable. And when researchers come to the library, I help them find what they need. We just had a huge collection of maps donated to the university and I'm in charge of cataloging them."

"That sounds interesting," he said.

"You are such a liar," Nan teased as she took her coffee away from him. "It sounds boring. You thought I was an old lady."

"I was gravely mistaken. And you set me straight on that."

She wrapped her arms around her knees, holding the warm coffee between her hands. "Your job is so much more exciting. People scream and clap for you. You make people cry when you sing. I bring people musty old books and make them sneeze."

"Well, if you could do something different, what would you do?"

Nan leaned back into the pillows and sighed. Though

she was naked from the waist up, she had no thought to cover herself. She was completely comfortable with Riley. And thrilled when he looked at her body with such obvious appreciation.

"When I was younger I wanted to be a heroine. Like Jane Eyre or Elizabeth Bennet. Before that, it was a princess. I lived inside books so I figured working in a library was a good choice for me." She paused, wondering how much more she could reveal without appearing completely ridiculous. But this was Riley. He seemed to accept her exactly the way she was. "I wrote a children's book last year."

"You did? What's it about?"

"About a monster that lives in a little girl's closet. After my mother died, I used to be so afraid to go to bed, afraid that I'd wake up the next morning and my whole world would be changed." She paused. "My mom died in the middle of the night and my dad woke me up in the morning to tell me."

Riley slipped his hand around her nape and pulled her into a soft kiss. "I'm sorry."

Nan smiled. "Before she got really sick, she used to sit and read to me every night before I fell asleep. And before she walked out of the room, she'd tell all the monsters to go away and come back another day." She shrugged. "It's just a silly story. I don't have any illustrations for it. I'm not very good at art."

"You could find someone to illustrate it. Danny went to art school."

"Is he an illustrator?"

Riley shook his head. "He studied sculpting. But I'm sure he'd know someone to contact."

"He must know how to draw if he went to art school."

"I've never really seen him draw, except when he does his designs. He makes iron fences and gates and andirons. And these wild sculptures fashioned out of junk. People from all over the world commission him to work for them. He's kind of famous."

"As famous as you?"

"With a different crowd," Riley replied. "His fans are all really rich people with big houses. Mine are all drunkards and pub rats."

"I'm your fan," she murmured, reaching out to slip her fingers beneath the waistband of his jeans.

"Come on, now. Get yourself up out of bed and into the shower. We have a busy day ahead."

"I think jet lag is starting to set in."

"You've had four nights to recover. I'm starting to believe you're just a layabout." He grabbed her coffee and set it on the bedside table, then threw the covers back and scooped her naked body up into his arms. "Shower first, then breakfast."

"No," Nan cried. Being with Riley was much easier without clothes, since he always seemed to be determined to take them off.

When they reached the bathroom, he turned on the shower and waited for the water to warm, then gently pushed her inside. "That will wake you up."

But Nan wasn't about to lose her advantage. Grabbing the front of his jeans, she unzipped them, then shoved them down over his hips. "Don't you want to join me?"

"Nan, that shower is like a bleedin' coffin. It barely fits one, much less two."

"It will be fun trying, though."

He kicked out of his jeans and stepped inside, pulling the curtain shut behind him. "See, I told you. Cramped quarters."

Their bodies were pressed so closely together beneath the water that just the slightest movement became incredibly erotic. "Can you reach the soap?" she asked.

He wrapped his arms around her and grabbed the soap, then struggled to put it in her hand. "Maybe if we swapped places," Riley said, gripping her waist and trying to turn them both around.

But as they moved, Riley backed against the shower curtain. Off balance, Nan bumped into him and he began to fall back into the curtain, which was caught under his foot. He reached out to steady her, but Nan was in no position to help him regain his footing.

The rod popped off the top of the shower and in a tangle of arms and legs, they fell onto the bathroom floor, their slippery bodies skidding on the vinyl curtain. The scene was so utterly ridiculous that all Nan could do was laugh.

Riley growled. "Look at what we've done. I'm going to have to take this out of your deposit."

"It wasn't my fault. You're the one who fell."

"You're the one who insisted I join you, even after I warned you it wouldn't work."

She lay on top of him, wriggling her hips against his

in a provocative way. "Oh, poor thing. It is such a hard-ship to take off your clothes and have a shower with a naked and willing woman. Whatever will you do?"

Riley grinned. "Willing? Willing to do what?"

Nan leaned close and pressed a kiss to the center of his damp chest. "I don't know. What do you have in mind?"

He was already hard and he moved beneath her, his shaft rubbing against her belly. "I'm sure if we lie here for a little while longer, something will come to us."

"WHERE ARE WE GOING?"

"To Bantry," Riley said as they strode along the wa-terfront in Ballykirk. "We don't have a lot of time, but the weather is fine, so I thought we'd go by water in-stead of driving."

"Really. We're going on a boat?"

"We're going to go on this boat," he said, pointing to a small fishing vessel tied up at the end of a weathered dock. Riley untied the stern line and tossed it onto the deck. "Hop on."

He helped Nan on board, then stepped into the tiny wheelhouse and started the engine. Nan stood next to him, watching everything he did with curious eyes.

"Is this your boat?"

"No, it belongs to my uncle. It's an old boat he re-stored, one that my great-grandfather used for the family fishing business. It's too small to use for com-mercial fishing now, but the family uses it for fun."

She ran her hand along the gleaming brightwork. "It's beautiful."

"I have to get the bow line. Open that locker there and grab a mack and a life jacket." Riley slipped past her and tossed off the last line to the quay, then returned to the cabin. He carefully maneuvered the boat away from the pilings and headed out into the harbor.

Nan pulled on the mackintosh, but it was so huge she looked ridiculous. She held her arms out, her hands completely hidden by the oilskin. Riley chuckled. "There has to be a smaller one in there. Give that one to me."

She slipped out of it, then searched the locker and came out with a jacket more her size. Riley helped her fasten the life jacket over the mack, then put on the larger size. "Now, Wellies," he said.

"Wellies." She peered into the locker and pulled out a pair of rubber boots. "Wellies?"

He nodded. Though they were usually worn over stocking feet, she pulled the pair on right over her shoes. Riley nodded as she did a model's turn in front of him.

"How do I look?" she asked.

"Adorable."

He'd been with a lot of women over the past ten years, and some of them he'd liked a lot. But he'd never met anyone quite as game as Nan. No matter what he suggested they do, she seemed to take it in stride, happy to simply spend the day in his company.

He'd always wondered how his parents had managed to make such a success of marriage. But now, he realized that they loved to spend time with each other. It didn't matter what they were doing, as long as they were doing it together. That's what it was like with Nan. Easy, relaxed, with nothing but fun in front of them.

Riley navigated out of the harbor at Ballykirk, then turned inland into Bantry Bay. As the boat chugged on, he scanned the coastline, searching the gray rocks for movement. When he finally caught it, he pointed. "Look. Seals."

Nan stepped out onto the deck, bracing her hands on the rail. "Right there," she cried, jumping up and down in childish delight. "Oh, look, there's a baby, too." She glanced over her shoulder at him. "Can we get closer?"

"Not here, it's too shallow," Riley said. "But maybe a bit farther down the coast."

She came back into the cabin and wrapped her arms around his waist. "I didn't realize there were seals in Ireland."

"They're the stuff of legends here. Haven't you ever heard of selkies?"

"No," she said. "There wasn't anything in my guide-books about that. Tell me."

"Well, by day, selkies are seals. They swim in the sea and sun on the rocks. But at night, they shed their skins and become human. Not just average humans, but extraordinarily beautiful men and women, seductive, with dark hair and pale skin. Ordinary people see them and they instantly fall in love. But the only way to keep a selkie is to find their skin, which they always carefully hide after they come out of the sea. If you can hide a selkie's skin, then you can keep them human."

"And are they happy together, the humans and the selkies?"

He shook his head. "A selkie will always long for the sea. They're drawn to it, to the beaches and the cliffs and the crashing waves on the shore. At night, they stand on the shore, their sad songs drifting out on the sea breeze."

"Can they ever go back?" Nan asked.

"Only if they find their skin. And then, once they go back, they can never return again. They still watch over their children though and are said to swim with them when they're in the water. They say that children of a selkie have the dark hair and pale skin of that parent, but they also have webs between their fingers and toes."

"I love that story," she said.

"Oh, there are many tales of selkies," he said. "Some of them very romantic and very tragic. My da used to tease us that my ma was a selkie. We were never really sure if it was the truth until we got a little older. Once, my little brother and I tore the house apart looking for her skin. She was furious at us, but my da was the one who got the punishment for telling us the tale."

"I can understand how you'd believe him. I believe you and I know for a fact that seals can't become humans."

He held up his hand. "See. There's a slight webbing there."

They searched the coast together and found more seals. Riley got closer to the shore and a few of the more curious animals swam near the boat. "They're not afraid," he explained. "Ireland is a sanctuary for seals and whales and dolphins. So they don't have to worry about hunters or fishermen."

Riley picked up an empty bucket from the deck. "Here. Bump this on the side of the boat. They'll think you're dumping bait and they might swim closer."

"Can we feed them?"

He shook his head. "It's not a good idea. They'll turn into beggars and spend all their time on the docks looking for tourists to feel them."

"Like the sheep on the pass?"

He nodded. "But they recognize the fishing boats and they'll come out looking for discarded bait. There are harbor dolphins in the bay, too. And out in the Atlantic, you can see whales this time of year."

"It's all so beautiful," she said. She pushed up on her toes and gave him a kiss on the cheek. "Thank you for showing it to me."

They pulled into Bantry Harbor an hour later, after exploring the coastline and following a pair of dolphins through the water. Riley helped Nan out of her boating wardrobe before leaving the boat for dry land.

"It's a market day, today," Riley explained. "You'll need to know that all prices are negotiable and if they think you're a tourist, they'll expect you to pay full price."

As they walked along the quay toward the quaint market district, Riley was greeted by some of the locals, fishermen and farmers who sold him their wares for the pub. They all insisted on introductions to Nan, engaging her in small talk as they tried to convince her to buy.

As they strolled, they listened to a few of the local musicians—an old man playing Beatles songs on a battered piano and a boy singing songs to an out-of-tune guitar. Riley grabbed a handful of coins from his pocket and dropped them in the boy's guitar case, then nodded. "Keep at it, lad. You sound grand."

Nan smiled at him as they continued up the street. "That was nice," she said.

"I used to come here to market day with my folks and they'd let me busk for a few hours. It used to kill my brothers when I came home with a punt or two and all I had to do for it was sing." He pointed to a pub with outdoor seating. "They have the best sausage sandwiches in all of County Cork. Why don't we have a bite and then we'll walk up to the gardens."

They found an empty table and Riley ordered them a few pints of Guinness and a couple of sandwiches. Nan must have been hungrier than she let on, because she devoured the sandwich in a matter of minutes. He ordered another, then watched her eat from across the table.

"We have sausage like this in Wisconsin. Bratwurst," she said. "You'd like them. We cook them on a grill and then put them in beer and onions. I live near the football stadium and on game days my whole house smells like bratwurst." She smiled at him. "Have you ever been to America?"

Riley shook his head. "Never. But I'd like to see it. My manager says I should go there to perform, to Boston or Chicago."

"Chicago," she said. "That's just a few hours away from where I live. I could come and see you. Or you could come and stay with me and I could show you around." She glanced at their surroundings. "Although, I don't think I have sights like this to show you."

"I wouldn't be coming for the sights," Riley said. "I'd be coming to see you."

"We do have some interesting things. You can go to the top of the Sears Tower in Chicago. Although it isn't called the Sears Tower anymore. And we have a zoo in Madison. And I'd want to take you down to the terrace at the student union. Oh, and we could go to the House on the Rock. Or the Wisconsin Dells and ride the ducks."

Riley stared at Nan from across the table, his chin cupped in his hand, his fingers slowly turning the beer glass in front of him. He loved to listen to her talk, even if it was about something he didn't understand. A house on a rock? Riding ducks?

There were times when he wanted to crawl inside her head and know everything she knew and feel everything she felt. What did she think of him? Was she as infatuated with him as he was with her?

"What are these potatoes?" she asked, holding out a forkful before popping it in her mouth. "I'm going to look like a potato when I leave here, all round and doughy."

"That's boxty," he said.

She took a bite of the boxty, then rolled her eyes. "Oh, this is so good. It's like hash browns mixed with mashed potatoes. This would be really good with a little garlic. Or maybe some onions?"

He continued to watch her enjoy her meal, but his thoughts focused only on the words she'd just spoken.

When I leave here. He knew she was scheduled to leave in five days. He'd promised to return her to the airport. But as they spent more time together, Riley found himself trying to come up with excuses for her to stay. There just wasn't enough time.

"If you wanted to stay a few days longer, you could," Riley said, trying to bring up the subject casually. "The cottage isn't booked for the rest of the summer."

"I'm on a budget. Ten days was all I could afford."

"You wouldn't have to pay," he said. "You'd be my guest."

"I wish I could," Nan said. "It's already Friday. It seems like the time has flown by so quickly."

"After the show at the pub tomorrow night, my schedule is completely yours."

"You don't have to do that," Nan said. "I didn't expect a personal tour guide twenty-four hours a day."

He picked up her hand and wove his fingers through hers, then kissed the inside of her wrist. "I think I'm a little more than that," he murmured.

A wicked little grin curved the corners of her mouth. "I've enjoyed our adventures in the bedroom. And yes, you are more than a tour guide."

"I like showing you around. I'm helping you avoid all the cheesy tourist spots."

"Where are we going tomorrow?" she asked. "Wait, no. I don't want to know. You can surprise me."

"I'll think of something good to do. I have band rehearsal in the afternoon, but we can spend the morning together. And we might have a ring from Carey Findley." Riley picked up his fork and scooped up some of the boxty and fed it to her. "Tell me about your life at home in…"

"Madison," she said. "Madison, Wisconsin. It's a big college town. There's a huge university there. I live in a little bungalow, the house that I grew up in."

"What about friends?"

"Are you asking about boyfriends?"

Riley shrugged. Of course that's what he was asking about. "Is there anyone back home you've been dating?"

"There is this guy at the library. Larry. We've been out a few times. But…"

"Larry? No, you can't be with a guy named Larry. Larry wears sensible shoes and thick glasses and carries his lunch in a briefcase. He drives an ugly car and likes to tend his lawn for a craic."

"Craic," she said. "Translation please."

"Good time," he said.

"And you."

"*I'm* a craic," he said.

She laughed. But Riley didn't think she was taking any of the conversation seriously. To her it was all just amusing chat. "Yes, you are."

"Feck Larry," he muttered beneath his breath.

"I used to think, if I really wanted to get married I could marry him. He's a nice guy and he has a good job. He loves books so we have that in common. But now, I think not."

"Hell no."

Nan giggled, nodding her head. "Hell no! You've ruined me for all other men. I'll never find anyone quite like you."

"Then don't," Riley said, turning serious. "Stay here and you won't have to."

"You know I can't do that."

"You can do anything you want," he countered.

"Can I tear off all your clothes right now?"

"No. I'm afraid they'd toss us out before you had a chance to finish your potatoes."

"I rest my case," she said. "I love these potatoes. I'm developing a much deeper appreciation of the common spud since I've been in Ireland."

Riley cursed beneath his breath. He fought the urge to tell her how he felt, to express to her how much he loved being with her. But every time he even broached the subject, she found a way to diffuse the emotion behind his words.

Maybe it would be better saved for a quiet moment in the bedroom. After all, they'd only known each other less than a week. That was plenty of time to realize that something very special was happening between them. He at least wanted her to acknowledge it.

They would have to have a serious talk tonight. He didn't want her to leave on Wednesday. Hell, he didn't want her to leave at all. And he wasn't going to be satisfied until she understood exactly where he stood.

NAN LOVED the market day in Bantry. The atmosphere was lively and the stalls colorful. There were vendors with fresh produce and fragant cheeses, salty olives and savory pastries, so many things to tempt her. Before long, she and Riley were lugging around bags of items she'd felt compelled to purchase.

They made a trip back to the boat, packing the perishables away in a cool spot before heading back for more. Though they'd meant to visit a large estate at the edge of town, Nan was determined to find the perfect memento to represent her trip to Ireland before it was too late. She'd looked in Killarney and in Ballykirk, but nothing had struck her fancy.

She pulled Riley to a stop in front of a small clothing store and stared at a hand-painted scarf in the window. "Look at that," she said. It was a colorful map of Ireland printed on a silk scarf, the kind of thing she could frame rather than wear. "That's pretty."

"Pretty ghastly," he said. "Isn't that something an old lady would wear?"

"No, I'd frame it. I love maps."

"Then buy a real map. There's a great bookshop in Ennis that sells antique maps. I can take you there."

"Will we have time before I leave?" Nan asked.

Riley cursed beneath his breath. "Do we always have to be talking about you going home?"

"I want to find the perfect memory," she said. "I'm going to go in and look at it. Maybe they have some others."

"I'll wait out here," he said.

"You don't want to come with me?"

"I'm not a big one for browsing for ladies' things," he said. "Unless, of course, you're shopping for lingerie. Then I'd be happy to be of assistance."

Nan laughed. "There's a pub across the street. Go get yourself a half-pint and I'll join you when I'm done."

"You won't be long?"

"Fifteen minutes at the most. And then we'll go to the gardens."

She watched as Riley started off across the street, then turned and entered the small shop. A bell rang above her head as she opened the door and the shop-keeper smiled at her from behind a small counter.

"Hello, there," the shopkeeper said. "It's a lovely day outside, isn't it?"

"Yes," Nan said. "Perfect."

"Is there anything I can help you find, then?"

"I noticed the scarf in the window," Nan said. "Do you have any others like it?"

"Oh, yes. Several," she said, pointing into the display case. "These are one-of-a-kind, you know. Hand-painted by a local artist. Let me show you."

As she looked through the scarves, Nan realized nothing she could buy would ever be perfect because they were only reminders of the land and scenery. Her most vivid memory of Ireland would always be Riley. Maybe she needed to buy something to create that one perfect memory of him.

"Do you carry lingerie?" she asked.

"I'm afraid we don't. We have some dressing gowns."

"Is there any place in town that has lingerie?"

"Burkes," she said. "They're a larger department store just around the corner."

Nan thanked the shopkeeper, then hurried back outside, glancing at her watch. She had ten minutes left before she'd agreed to meet Riley at the pub. She could run in and out and come away with something sexy.

Burkes was a large store with a beautiful red facade

of arched display windows. She hurried inside, then asked for directions to the lingerie department. But along the way, a pretty pale green cotton dress caught her eye. It had a deeply cut neck and back and a long, flowing skirt. Hand-crocheted lace decorated the neckline.

She wouldn't be able to wear a bra with it, which made it all the more provocative, and yet it wasn't too revealing. It was feminine and sexy, exactly the kind of thing she needed to wear to Riley's show. The kind of dress that would make him forget all the other women in the room and focus entirely on her.

"Can I try this on?" Nan asked, the lingerie forgotten.

"The dressing rooms are in the rear," the clerk said. "I'll be back to check on you in a moment."

After she closed the door behind her, Nan stripped out of her clothes and bra and pulled the dress over her head. The gauzy material was soft on her skin and clung to all her curves. The skirt came down to midcalf and yet was slit up to the thigh on one side.

"Perfect," she murmured, smiling at her reflection in the mirror. Nan spun around then examined the low back on the dress. Though she'd never gone out in public without a bra, there was no reason not to feel comfortable in the dress.

Facing the mirror, she examined her breasts and came away pleased with the overall impression. There were a few benefits to being slightly flat-chested.

Nan reached beneath the skirt and skimmed off her panties, then smiled. She could wear the dress with nothing underneath, she mused. Riley would probably enjoy that even more. She ran her fingers through her hair. Maybe a pretty thong would be better.

Nan winced. She'd never worn a thong in her life. They'd always looked so uncomfortable. And a bit too racy for her tastes. A knock sounded on the door. "Is there anything else I can get for you?" the salesclerk asked.

Nan poked her head out the door. "I need lingerie. Panties. Maybe a thong? Something lacy. White, I think."

A few minutes later, another knock sounded on the door and she opened it, only to find Riley standing outside. "Let me in," he whispered, a devilish grin on his face.

"No! You can't come in here."

"There's no one around. Come on, let me in."

"How did you find me?"

"I saw you from across the street. What's taking you so long?"

"Go away," she said. The salesclerk would be returning in a few minutes with her lingerie and any attempt at surprising him would be gone. Nan closed the door, but he knocked again. Frustrated, she let him in.

"Sit," she murmured. "And pull your feet up."

Riley did as he was told, wrapping his arms around his legs. "Pretty dress," he commented. "Are you wearing underwear?" He reached for the hem and peered beneath her skirt, but she slapped his hand away.

"Are you stark naked underneath that dress?"

"Yes."

"Oh, Jaysus, I shouldn't have come in here."

A third knock sounded at the door and Nan shushed him. She opened the door a crack and took the handful of hangers from the clerk. "Thanks," she murmured. "I'll be out in a few minutes."

"Oh, take all the time you need," the clerk said, as if she knew what was going on inside the room.

When she shut the door, Nan could feel her cheeks flushed from embarrassment.

"Oh, now, what's this?" Riley asked, pointing to the thongs.

"Stop," Nan said. "I just needed something to wear for tomorrow night. I didn't bring along anything pretty. I don't really own anything pretty." She smoothed her hands over the skirt. "Not like this."

"You'd look sexy in a potato sack."

"Since there are no potato sacks in this store, I'm going to have to settle for this dress," she said.

"I like it, but I don't approve of going without drawers."

"That's why I wanted to try the thongs."

"Well, look at these things," he said, taking the hangers from her hand. "You might as well go without."

"I thought you'd find it sexy," she said.

"Yeah, me and a hundred other blokes at the pub. I don't want my girl running around without her knickers. It sends the wrong message."

Nan took a slow breath as she toyed with the lace at

the neck, her gaze fixed on her reflection. "Do you like the dress?"

"I'd like it better if you wore a T-shirt underneath it."

"I can't believe you're so prudish," she said.

He stood up and wrapped his arms around her waist, then brushed a kiss across her lips. "Yes," he murmured. "I love the dress. I think you look incredible. With or without clothes." He pressed her back against the mirror, his hands wandering over the curves of her body, the fabric of the dress creating a delicious friction.

"Don't you think the clerk will be able to see that we're both in here?" She pointed to the space beneath the door. "She can see our feet."

"I'm sure this isn't the first time this changing room has been occupied by two." He kissed her neck. "I really like this dress."

"I do, too."

"Did you buy the scarf in the other store?"

Nan shook her head. "I didn't love it. I want to find something perfect."

Riley reached into his pocket and took out a small box. "Here. I found something that might do the trick."

Nan smiled. "What is this?"

"Open it," he insisted. "It's nothing grand, but it's very Irish."

She opened the box and pulled away the tissue paper to find a gold ring nestled inside. Nan took it out and looked at it, the design vaguely familiar.

"It's a claddagh," Riley explained, bending close, his

lips softly touching her cheek. "The heart is for love, the hands for friendship and the crown for loyalty."

"It's beautiful," she said, glancing up at him.

"Now, there's a trick to wearing it," he said. "And I'm not sure how it all goes. I suppose it doesn't really matter. Some people wear it as a wedding or engagement ring, I suppose on their left hand. So wear it on your right."

She slipped it on the ring finger of her right hand. "It fits perfectly."

"Well, that was a lucky guess," he said.

"Thank you," Nan murmured, holding her hand out to stare at the ring. "I love it. It's exactly what I was looking for."

"Good," he said. "I'm glad I was able to help." He drew a deep breath and nodded. "Well, I'll just be getting out of your way. I'll meet you outside then?"

She nodded. Nan opened the door and Riley looked both ways before stepping out. After she closed the door behind him, she sat down on the low bench and stared at the ring. Her heart fluttered and she tried to take a deep breath, but it was impossible.

What did this mean? Was it custom in Ireland to give a ring to someone you barely knew? Nan was hesitant to attach any sentiment to it beyond friendship, but that didn't stop her from wondering if he had other intentions in giving it to her.

Yes, it was Irish. And maybe that's all it was, Nan thought. But deep inside her, in the furthest corners of her heart, she wanted it to mean more.

6

RILEY SAT ON A STOOL on the small stage in the pub, plucking out a melody on his guitar. He glanced at the lyrics for the song he'd written, then cursed softly, frustrated with the tune he'd been working on.

Why was it that songs always sounded so much better inside his head than they did once he sang them out loud? There were times when he felt he'd come up with an idea so perfect, there was nothing better. And yet, the moment he tried to work it all out—the lyrics, the melody, the harmony beneath—it wasn't nearly as wonderful as he'd imagined.

This is exactly why artists self-destructed. There was nothing worse than facing your own inadequacies as a musician and he seemed to face them almost daily. But since Nan had arrived he'd felt even more conflicted about his career. For a long time he'd been perfectly satisfied with his life. And now, he saw his carefree, irresponsible existence for what it was—his inability to take life seriously.

Even if he wanted to fall in love with Nan, he

couldn't. What did he have to offer her? All his possessions could fit in the back of his car. He didn't hold a proper job or own a home. He didn't have a college degree or any prospects for a job that offered a regular paycheck. Hell, he wasn't qualified to do anything but tend bar and sing songs.

His mind flashed back to the previous day, to their encounter in the dressing room at Burkes. Riley stifled a groan. Could he have made more of a bollocks of the gift than he had? What had ever possessed him to pull it out and give it to her then? And why pretend it meant nothing beyond friendship when he knew it didn't?

The moment he'd seen the ring in the shop window, he knew it was exactly what he wanted to give Nan. It represented all the feelings he had for her, all wrapped up in a shiny bit of gold. There was friendship first and then loyalty. And now, there was this growing sense of something more. He wasn't sure if it was love, at least not yet. But it felt an awful lot like something serious.

If he knew anything about Nan, he knew she was a practical girl and not the type to believe in love at first sight. They'd met each other on a Monday and today was Saturday. Five days and nights. How was anyone supposed to know how they felt after so short a time?

Hell, he knew how much he wanted her, how her touch drove him wild every time they were together. And how her naked body felt against his as they lost themselves in each other. But that was lust, not love. And he had no doubts at all about those feelings.

After their trip to Bantry yesterday, they'd gone back to the cottage and prepared a dinner of salmon and fresh vegetables. For dessert, they'd indulged in an apple tart that Nan had bought from a baker at the fair. It was a long, lazy meal followed by a slow, delicious seduction. And in Riley's mind, it was life exactly as it should be lived.

He'd never really thought about falling in love and what it would mean to his life. But he liked evenings alone with Nan. And mornings bringing her coffee. And everything in between. For the first time, he could imagine what married life might be like.

He sighed softly, then turned his attention back to the song he was working on. But a few moments later, the Unholy Trinity walked in the front door, chattering about the recent decision to replace the streetlamps in Ballykirk. They sat down at the bar and Riley set his guitar back on its stand and wandered over to serve them.

"What are you lads up to today?" he asked, dropping a cardboard coaster in front of each of them.

"Streetlamps. What in the name of all that's holy do we need with new lamps?" Dealy asked. "I'm all for modernization, but I happen to remember when they put those lamps in. It was 1968, it was. Over forty damn years ago."

"They use too much electricity," Markus said. "They way I hear it, these new lamps will pay for themselves in ten years."

"Oh, and then we'll need new ones because they'll discover a way to run streetlamps on the lint stuck inside your navel."

Riley chuckled. "I assume this discussion requires a full pint for each of you."

They all nodded and Riley turned to pull them each a glass of Guinness. "Say, you lads have been around Ballykirk for a long time. Do you remember a bloke named Carey Findley? Jimmy McPhee says he used to live out on a farm on the way to Glengarriff."

"Oh, yes," Johnnie said. "Carey Findley. He's my second cousin twice removed. He lives near Kealkill now. Moved off the farm after his son was drowned."

Riley swallowed hard. "Drowned?"

"Tragic story, that," Johnnie said, shaking his head. "He was a wild boy, hard to control. Got in a lot of trouble, he did."

"How did he die?" Riley asked.

"He was out with some friends on the bay in a small boat and one of the boys fell in. The water was cold and he had trouble and the Findley boy went in after him. They both went under and didn't come up again. After that, Carey couldn't live near the water. Moved to a place just outside Kealkill. Heard his wife died after that. Brokenhearted, she was."

"Oh, God," Riley murmured.

"That was years ago. How long, Dealy? Thirty years?"

"Twenty-seven," Riley said.

"Yes. That's right," Johnnie said. "It happened a few months after my youngest girl was born. She was sick with a fever and we couldn't go to the wake. He was buried with his mother's family in Glengarriff, if I recall."

"What's he to you?" Markus asked.

"There was a photo of him and some of his friends on the wall over there. I was just curious."

"He used to come into the pub a lot. Was quite a charmer, that one. Always looking for a pretty girl."

"That's what I heard," Riley said. He drew a deep breath and rested his hands on the bar. "Katie's got a tasty stew going for lunch today. Can I interest you in a bowl or two?"

"Oh, that would be grand," Dealy said. "And where is the cute little colleen of yours?"

"She's wandering about town," Riley said as he walked toward the kitchen. "I'm off to find her right now." When he got inside the kitchen, Riley found Danny sitting at one of the prep tables, reading a newspaper and drinking a mug of coffee. "Have you come to work?" he asked as he handed Katie the order.

"Right after I eat," his brother said. "I figured you'd want the day to spend with your girl."

"She's not my girl," he said. "Not officially."

"Do you want it to be official?" Danny asked.

"Hell, I don't know. I don't want her to go home. But I'm not sure if that's because I'm falling in love with her or because the sex is crazy good."

"I'm not hearin' this," Katie said from behind them both. She put her hands over her ears. "Leave my kitchen with your talk of sin and sex."

"Katie, girl, you've had three children. Certainly you know about how it all works in the bedroom," Danny teased.

"Yes, but I'm married and you're not. And I have

three daughters, although thankfully, you'll never get near them. You both need to go to confession."

Danny picked up his paper and his mug and walked out the back door, Riley following him. They walked around to the front of the pub and sat down on a bench near the front door. "What are you going to do about this girl?" Danny asked.

"I don't know," Riley said. "I have to find some way to get her to stay."

"Have you thought about going home with her? It wouldn't be a bad way to see America."

"Yeah. But there's not a lot I can offer her. You know, women love musicians, but they don't want to marry them, at least not those of us who spend our weekends in pubs filled with drunken girls."

"You make more than most," Danny said, "And if you focused on writing songs and producing, you'd make even more. Hell, how much do you need? You've got enough saved to buy a decent house."

"She deserves more than a decent house. She deserves a grand house and fine clothes and no worries for the rest of her life."

"Are you even sure that's what she wants?" Danny asked. "She doesn't seem like the type to care about things like that."

"Isn't that what every woman wants?"

"I think the point of being in love is that you want each other and the rest of it takes care of itself."

Riley leaned forward, bracing his elbows on his knees. "Wouldn't that be nice if it were that simple."

"Maybe you should just stop worrying about this

and let it happen," Danny suggested. "If she doesn't love you, you can't force her to. And you're not sure how you feel."

"Don't you wonder if you might have missed a chance at something good because you weren't playing attention or you just didn't give it enough time?"

Danny shook his head. "The way I see it, love shouldn't be that fragile that it hinges on simple circumstances. It's tough and resilient and once you find it, it doesn't go away easily. It's always there."

"Have you ever been in love?"

"No. But that's the way I imagine it to be."

Riley stood up, shoving his hands into his pockets. "I have to go. You'll keep an eye on the pub? The Unholy Trinity is in there waiting for lunch."

"Don't jump the gun on this, Riley," Danny warned. "The last thing you want is to convince her to stay then realize that you don't really love her at all. It would be a cruel thing, that."

Riley started off down the street. Nan had decided to spend the morning exploring Ballykirk on her own, anxious to visit the church and few of the shops. He'd agreed to meet her for a picnic lunch and a drive along the coast before he had to be back for rehearsal.

If the time was right, he'd try again to convince her to stay. It wasn't that difficult to change a plane ticket, and she still hadn't learned much about her mother. And there were so many sights they hadn't seen. Given the rest of the day, he could probably come up with more reasons for her to delay her departure, but for now, that was enough.

THE PUB WAS PACKED with barely enough room to move. Riley had saved a seat for Nan next to Martin, his moody cousin, and the band's sound technician. Nan felt relieved she didn't have to try to watch from the midst of the crush and had a nice little elevated perch from which to see the stage.

She had to wonder where the crowd had come from. Ballykirk was such a small village. But everyone in attendance seemed to be familiar with the band, dancing and shouting out names and singing along with the lyrics.

As the evening went on, the crowd became more and more boisterous and the music more raucous. She'd known Riley as the sweet and sexy guy who spent his nights in her bed and his days driving her all over Ireland. But when he was on stage, she got a chance to see a different side of him.

From the moment he began singing, he had the audience under his spell. Like a lover, he teased and seduced them with his songs, making them want more. He smiled and joked and charmed. And with each song, he built toward a frenzy of energy and music that made her want to jump up and dance. The lively tunes, the playful lyrics, the fiddle and the penny whistle, it was all so much good fun.

Though she knew she was probably imagining things, Riley seemed to be singing every song to her, their gazes meeting across the room. When she waved at him, he'd smile. The band finally left the stage after a rousing rendition of a Pogues song that left the audience exhausted, yet satisfied. But Riley stayed on stage, sitting down on a stool with an acoustic guitar.

"This is a song for a beautiful lady from America. It's a song I wrote especially for her and this is the first time I'm going to play it. I hope you like it."

Nan leaned forward, her elbows on the sound table, her eyes fixed on Riley as he spun the tale of a man in love with a beautiful selkie. The way he sang the ballad, it was as if he were singing about the two of them, and their fated relationship.

Nan watched him, amazed at the depth of emotion he conveyed to the audience…and to her. She barely knew Riley, and even though they'd been more intimate than she'd ever been with a man before, she didn't know the tiny details of his life. But, as she watched him, she felt a certain sense of pride in his talent and a fierce attachment.

This was the man who'd chosen to share her bed, this was the man that every girl in the room was lusting after. And tonight, she'd go home with him, she'd take his clothes off and lie naked beside him. A shiver skittered through her body, the anticipation causing an intense physical response.

Riley sang two more songs, both of them sweet love songs, before he nodded to the crowd and stepped off stage, a bottle of beer dangling from his fingers. He headed directly to the control table, but his trip was interrupted again and again by enthusiastic fans—mostly female.

When he finally reached her, he glanced back over his shoulder and took her hand. "Come on, let's get out of here. I need some air." She stood and he leaned closer. "I need some you."

They walked out the front door, into the cool night, and Nan wrapped her arm around his as they strolled aimlessly toward the waterfront. The sounds from the pub faded and when they were finally alone, she spoke. "You were so good. I was just so impressed."

"That I can sing?"

"No, I knew you could sing. You sang that song for me the first night we were together. And I loved the song about the selkie," Nan said. "It was so sad. But you have this way with the audience. You draw them in. And they can't help but love you."

"And you?"

"I love you, too," Nan said, only realizing the meaning of her words after they'd been said.

There were a few people wandering along the quay and they all recognized Riley and said hello. He found a spot for them to sit, then took a long sip of his beer, staring out at the water, his expression turning serious.

Nan felt a nervous twist in her stomach. She shouldn't have said that to him. He must have misunderstood. It wasn't that she loved *him*. She loved the person he was on stage, singing to her. "What's wrong?" she asked, ready to hear the typical excuses. She shouldn't get too attached. She'd be going home soon. They were moving too fast. "I'm sorry. I shouldn't have said that."

"Said what?" he asked.

"Th-that I…loved you. It came out wrong."

He chuckled. "That's not it. I like that you said that."

"Then why do you look so serious?"

He drew a deep breath and let it out slowly. "Today, at the pub, I asked the Unholy Trinity if they remembered Carey Findley. And Johnnie O'Malley knew a little more about Tiernan."

"What about Tiernan?"

Riley paused. "As Johnnie remembers, Tiernan died shortly after your mother left Ireland."

She stared at him, her eyes wide, her expression stunned. "How?"

"He drowned in the bay a few months after your mom went home. He was trying to save a friend. And I called Carey Findley again this afternoon and he'd like to see you. He remembers your mom. And from what he told me, she and Tiernan had a thing."

Nan suddenly felt as if the world was closing in on her, all the oxygen suddenly sucked out of the atmosphere. Though she tried to draw a deep breath, she couldn't. "Were they in love?"

"I'm not sure. But considering she named you after him, I think it might be possible."

"No, no. I don't want to hear this," Nan said, covering her ears. "I don't want to hear that she fell in love and then had to leave him. Or that she fell in love and then he died. I don't want this to be a sad story. Her life was sad enough."

"You don't have to go see him," Riley said. "You don't have to do anything if you don't want to."

"Yes, I do. Now that I know where he is, I have to go. I need to find out about the letters he wrote to my mother. I need to know more about her. And about Tiernan."

Riley shook his head. "Not if it's going to make you unhappy."

"Well, sometimes life isn't all butterflies and daisies. Sometimes life just sucks. Don't you think I know that? We can pretend that everything is fine between us, but we both know I'm going to have to leave and we'll never see each other again."

"You don't have to leave. I told you that you could stay."

"That's not the point!" Nan said. "I came all this way to find out more about my mother and I can't just let it go."

"I'm sorry," Riley said, a trace of frustration creeping into his voice. "Are we talking about us or your mother?"

Nan paced back and forth in front of him. Everything was all jumbled in her head. Was this really about her mother or was it about her feelings for Riley? Nan didn't want to believe her mother had walked away from the boy she loved, or that she'd be forced to do the same. "I'm not sure." She plopped down beside him. "Maybe she loved him. And maybe she decided that wasn't enough, that she had to go home. Maybe she made the wrong decision."

"She married your father. They must have been in love," Riley said.

"He was so much older than her," Nan said. "Almost fifteen years."

"He was a man, Tiernan was a boy. Your father was at home and Tiernan was here, far away from everything your mother knew. It's not hard to understand her choice."

She turned back to him. "I'm going home," she said.

"To the cottage?"

She ran her hands through her hair, her cheeks rosy from the chilly night. "I need some time to think."

"Come on, Nan. Come back to the pub. You'll listen to some music and have a drink and—"

"I'll see you later," she said, starting down the street. As she passed the pub, Nan picked up her pace, running toward the road that led to the cottage. Before long, she was breathless, gasping, a stitch cramping her side. But she didn't stop moving, her retreat the only thing she could focus on.

Why had she even come to Ireland? What kind of naive fool had she been, thinking there'd be some fairy-tale story waiting for her here? Life wasn't a fantasy, it was real and it was full of pain and disappointment.

And now, she was making the same mistake her mother had made, falling for a handsome Irish man, letting desire rule her heart instead of common sense ruling her head. How easy it was to fall under the spell of this place and to believe in the magic.

After climbing the hill to the cottage, she ran up the garden path and threw open the cottage door, then stood in the middle of the dark room, drawing in deep gulps of air. With a groan, her legs buckled beneath her and she sat down on the floor and buried her face in her hands.

Could she bear to leave him? Riley was the only man she'd ever truly wanted. He'd changed the way she thought about herself and about her future. And without him, she'd go back to being just an ordinary woman. Nan angrily brushed away the tears, refusing to feel sorry for herself.

She got to her feet and strode into the bathroom, then splashed cold water on her face. "Stop it!" she scolded. As she looked at her reflection in the mirror, she barely recognized the woman staring back at her.

This place had changed her, in less than a week she'd become a different person. She was falling in love with Riley Quinn and all the commonsense warnings she gave herself didn't mean anything. He'd found a place in her heart and she was willing to turn her life upside down just to believe in the fantasy.

She grabbed a tissue and blew her nose, then wandered out to the sofa. Curling up on one end, Nan pulled a pillow tightly to her body. But then the front door slammed against the wall and she jumped to her feet at the sound.

Riley stood in the opening, his wild gaze fixed on her, his body tense. Then, in a few short steps he'd crossed the room and pulled her into his arms.

She didn't have time to resist. In truth, she didn't want to. When his mouth came down on hers, Nan felt her anger melt away and her heart surrender to his touch. His hands skimmed over her body, as if he were reassuring himself that she was still his, that he still had the capacity to make her moan.

"I'm sorry," he murmured, cupping her face in his hands and murmuring his apology against her lips. "I never meant to hurt you and I should never have stuck my nose into this. It wasn't my place."

"No, I'm sorry. You were just trying to help and I was ungrateful."

"Tell me we're all right," he said, an edge of desperation in his voice.

Nan nodded. Her feelings for him had grown so powerful that she was willing to ignore her doubts and insecurities. Her mother might have made a mistake leaving Ireland all those years ago. But nothing about her relationship with Riley felt like a mistake. She was in love with him and she didn't want to deny feelings that felt so right.

He tore at her clothes, exposing bare skin to his lips and his hands. But it wasn't enough, his need to possess her nearly overwhelming them both. They stumbled into the bedroom and he pulled his shirt off over his head.

Pressing her against the wall, Riley drew her thigh up along his leg, their hips creating a delicious friction that promised more pleasure to come. Nan reached for the buttons on the front of his jeans and undid them one by one, and Riley groaned softly with every movement of her hand.

When she finally freed him to her touch, he sighed softly, leaning into her as she stroked. As he whispered his need, his breath warm on her temple, Riley drew her skirt up around her waist and, pushing aside her thong, found the moist folds of her desire.

For Nan, there was nothing more pleasurable than his touch, and nothing that gave her more exquisite torment. They were still clothed, but that only seemed to make their need more frantic as they searched for places to explore.

"I want to be inside you," Riley murmured breathlessly.

"Yes" was all Nan needed to say.

He wrapped her legs around his waist and carried her to the bed, then found a condom where they'd left them the night before, on the bedside table. In a heartbeat, he was sheathed and ready, and then slowly thrusting himself into her wet heat.

Nan was so close that it took only a few strokes before she dissolved into shudders and spasms. Riley was with her, his orgasm coming right on top of hers until they were both gasping and groaning together.

It had taken all of four or five minutes from the moment he'd thrown open the door to the instant they both lost control, but it was still one of the most powerful sexual experiences that Nan had ever had.

"I don't want to go back to the pub," he murmured.

Nan pushed up on her elbow. "What?"

"Yeah, I left the lads to fend for themselves. But they're going to run out of songs in another five or ten minutes." He drew her into a long, delicious kiss. "Do you want to come with me?"

She curled her body into his. "I think I'll stay here. But you'll come back?"

"You'd have to drag me out to sea to keep me away," he said. Riley ran his fingers through her short-cropped hair. "Don't ever doubt my feelings for you, Nan. They're as real as they can be."

"Go then," she said with a playful pout, "but come back as soon as you can."

He restored order to his clothes, then gave her a quick kiss. "I'll be back," he said.

"And I'll be naked," she replied with a playful smile.

Riley groaned as he walked out of the bedroom. "How am I supposed to concentrate on my songs now?"

RILEY ROLLED OVER in the bed, sliding his hand out to search for Nan's naked body. Rubbing at his sleepy eyes, he pushed up to find her side of the bed empty. "Nan?"

The cottage was silent. The scent of freshly brewed coffee permeated the air. He crawled out of bed and made his way to the kitchen, not bothering with clothes. But to his surprise, he found his brother Kellan rummaging through a cabinet next to the hearth.

"Jaysus, Kellan, what are you doing here? Where is Nan?"

"She's outside," Kellan said. "Having her coffee in the garden." He glanced over his shoulder and chuckled. "Put some clothes on, ya lazy git. I don't need to be staring at all your bits and pieces."

"What are you doing here?"

"I'm looking for one of my sketchbooks. I think I left it the last time I stayed."

Riley shook his head, then walked back to the bedroom to retrieve his jeans. He tugged them on, leaving the buttons open. "There's a blue notebook in the bottom drawer of the bedside table," he said, standing in the doorway.

Kellan levered to his feet and strode into the bedroom, brushing past his brother. A few moments later, he joined him at the bedroom door, a smile on his face. "Found it." He stared at Riley for a long moment, the shook his head. "Look at you. Aren't you a sight?"

Frowning, Riley ran his hand through his messy hair. "I just got up. I worked late last night."

"That's not what I meant. Take a look in the mirror, little brother. You're upside down over this girl and you don't even know it. And she's going to walk out of your life in a few days."

"So?" Riley shot back. "At least I'm out there looking. You haven't had a serious relationship since Fiona and that was what—three years ago? That torch you're dragging around is getting a wee bit heavy, isn't it?"

Kellan's jaw twitched and Riley waited for the inevitable sarcastic reply. But then his older brother drew a deep breath and shrugged. "You're right. You'd be a bleedin' eedjit not to see where this was all going. Who the hell knows? Maybe she'll stay."

"Maybe," Riley murmured.

Kellan patted his hand on Riley's shoulder. "I hope she does." He turned and walked to the door. "I'm headed back to Dublin. I'll see you next week."

"Next week," he said as he watched Kellan walk out the door. Then Riley leaned up against the doorjamb. Next week. Everything would go right back to normal next week. He'd actually liked his life before Nan had stumbled into it. But now, he knew there would be something missing once she left.

So he'd put more effort into convincing her to stay. And if she refused, he'd put more effort into dating.

He'd find a girl who was geographically available and he'd go after her. And if he were lucky, he'd find a girl he liked as much as Nan and they'd start a life together. This wasn't complicated. There were plenty of available women in Ireland.

Riley grabbed a mug of coffee and stepped out the front door. Kellan was chatting with Nan and they seemed to be on friendly terms for two relative strangers. "Sorry to barge in on your mornin'," Kellan said.

"I'm glad you found your notebook," Nan replied with a warm smile.

Kellan walked to the gate, then turned around and gave her a wave and a smile. Riley frowned at him, wondering at his brother's sudden change of personality. Kellan rarely smiled these days. "Get out of here," Riley shouted. "And don't be charming my girl."

"Feck off," Kellan said, chuckling to himself. "Nan, if you get weary of hanging around with this culchie, you ring me up. I'll show you a grand time."

Kellan hopped in his car and roared off down the road toward the village. Riley cursed him beneath his breath. He sat down on the garden bench next to Nan. "You'd best watch out for him. He's got the manners of a horny goat."

"He was very nice," Nan said. She reached out and ran her hand through Riley's hair, smoothing it out of his eyes. "You're awake."

"I had a very long night last night."

She leaned over and brushed a kiss over his lips. "I liked waking up to a naked man crawling into my bed," she said. "What time did you get back?"

"It was past two. I had my way with you and you fell right back to sleep."

Her cheeks flushed a pretty shade of pink. "Sorry."

"No problem." Riley met her gaze. "I'm sorry about last night. I didn't mean to stick my nose in where it didn't belong. You're right. These are your decisions to make and I'll stand behind whatever you want."

"I don't want to talk about it right now," she said. "I just want to enjoy this beautiful morning. Look at that water. Have you ever seen anything quite so lovely?"

Riley smiled. "Every time I look at you."

This brought a bubble of laughter. "Charm must run in the family."

He took a sip of his coffee. "We don't have a lot of these mornings left," he murmured.

"I know." Nan drew a deep breath of the clear morning air and smiled. "I needed this trip. I didn't realize how much until this moment. It's filled up my soul."

"What will you do when you get back?"

"Probably go right back to work. I've got my maps to catalog. They're really interesting. They were used in building the railroads, so they're some of the most detailed topographical maps of the time."

"Then you like your job?"

Nan nodded. "It's a good job. I do interesting work."

Riley forced a smile. No matter how he tried to figure this out in his head, it seemed more impossible with every day that passed. He reached out and took her hand, pressing her fingers to his lips.

She wore the ring he'd given her and he found a certain satisfaction in that. As long as she wore it, she wouldn't forget him. "I'm going to miss you when you leave."

"You like me, don't you?" she teased.

"Yes," Riley admitted. "I really like you."

She stared at him for a long moment, her head tipped to one side. "Maybe someday, I could come back. I mean, I don't expect you to wait around for that day. And I'll understand if you meet someone else. But if you don't, then maybe I could visit again."

"This would be the longest-distance relationship I've ever heard of," he said.

"It's not that far."

He shook his head slowly. "No, it isn't. When would you come again?"

"I don't know," Nan said with a shrug. "I get four weeks of vacation each year. Maybe sometime in the spring?"

Riley groaned and wrapped his arm around her shoulders. He nuzzled his face into the curve of her neck. "That's too far away," he said.

"We don't need to decide now. We can think about it later," Nan said.

Was that her reaction to every difficult decision she was faced with? She'll think about it later? When Riley saw something he wanted, he usually went after it without any hesitation. But Nan seemed to be the opposite, carefully considering each decision she made, giving herself time to mull it all over. What had happened to the carefree, spontaneous girl she'd first shown him?

Riley grabbed a daisy from beside the bench, snapping the stem and holding it up in front of her. "Tell me what you want to do today. It's Sunday so almost everyone in Ireland is in church. We won't be able to drive anywhere until the afternoon."

"Why?"

"A lot of times the roads are blocked by cars parked around the churches in some of the small villages. But we could drive to Cashel. It's an old ruin of a church and abbey set on a high hill. It's quite beautiful."

"That sounds good," she said. "But I'm going to drive. I think I've mastered the Fiat."

"Oh, no, we're not taking that piece of crap out on the road."

"Not a week ago you were telling me what a great car it was," Nan said. "You were extolling its virtues."

"I was full of shite," Riley said. "I suppose I have no choice but to let you drive my car."

"Really?" Nan asked.

"Yes. Really."

She stood up, quite pleased with herself. "All right. Just as along as we don't have to stop on any hills. I'm not good at that yet. And I can't drive in the cities at all. And if I wander on to the wrong side of the road, you have to tell me because sometimes I kind of forget."

Riley grabbed her hand and pulled her down on his lap. "You are really a giant pain in the arse, Nan Galvin."

"I know. But you'll just have to learn to deal with it," she teased. "At least for a few more days."

"I am. And it's not as bad as I thought it would be."

"Really?" she said, arching her eyebrow and looking at him quizzically. "Tell me what you were expecting."

"The last thing I expected to do was share your bed," he said. "I don't know. I had the picture of you in my head. You looked a little bit like my aunt Sally. You wore sensible shoes and little reading glasses that sat on the end of your nose."

"I'm sorry to disappoint," Nan said.

"Oh, sweetheart, don't ever think that. You had me the moment you walked out that door."

She curled up in his arms. "Would you like to know what I thought of you?"

"Before you met me?"

"Yes. I had this picture of a handsome Irishman with dark hair and pale eyes. Kind of scruffy but charming. A little dangerous, but with a kind heart. And I was right. I just never thought I'd be attracted to you."

"What was it then? The sexy smile or the witty personality?"

"It was your eyes," she said. "I thought you had the prettiest eyes I'd ever seen."

Riley cupped her face in his hands, staring at her for a long moment. God, there was no way he could deny it any longer. He'd fallen hopelessly in love with Nan. Sitting here in this garden, his life was perfect. There was nothing more that he needed to make himself happy.

He leaned forward and kissed her, his mouth lingering over hers. Riley wanted to say the words, to tell her how he really felt, but he knew she wasn't ready. There would still be time to make her want him as much as he wanted her. And he'd take every chance he found to make her see the truth in what he already knew in his heart.

Scooping her into his arms, he stood and carried her back to the cottage. "If you take me back to bed, I'm seriously going to wonder whether you only like me for the sex," Nan joked.

"I'm taking you to find your shoes, woman. You can't drive my car barefoot."

7

THE RUINS OF THE ABBEY at Cashel were more beautiful than Nan could have ever imagined, set high on the hill overlooking the plains all around. But after touring the ruins, Riley had insisted that they visit Athassel Priory, just a few miles away.

Once again, he'd brought them to another impossibly romantic spot. They'd left the car on the road and climbed over a gate, then trudged through a farmer's field to get to the ruined abbey. As Nan stood in the center of what was once the nave, she stared up at the high stone walls jutting into the blue sky.

The priory was nothing more than a shell, a ruin, yet it still had a beauty that she found breathtaking. Three arched Gothic windows were set in the center of the highest wall and she closed her eyes and tried to imagine what it looked like all those years ago. As she listened to the wind and the raucous cries of the jackdaws nesting in the holes in the walls, she felt the spirits of ancient Irishmen all around her.

She turned to look at Riley. He was standing in a

doorway, his hands braced on either side, staring out at the river that flowed near the abbey.

"Did Cromwell ruin this one, too?" she asked.

He stepped away from the door. "I don't think so. I think it burnt down before he got to Ireland."

They were all alone here, the chattering tourists with their cameras left behind at Cashel. Nan walked over to a stairway and peered through the bars that blocked the way. "Don't you wonder what it was like? Who lived here? What they did every day?"

Riley nodded. "I suppose I never thought much about it," he said. "These ruins are just part of the landscape here."

"I guess you don't really appreciate something you see every day," Nan said. "It's only interesting to strangers." She sent him a winsome smile. "I think that's why you find me so interesting."

He took her hand and they walked out the Gothic doorway into the cloisters that ran along one side of the church. There was so much history in this one spot that she found it difficult to take it all in.

Again and again, she was astounded at how this country had captured her imagination. Everywhere she looked, there was something pulling her in, as if she'd walked in these same footsteps in another life. Though her ancestors had come from this country, until she'd landed at Shannon, she'd never really given that a second thought.

"Do you believe in reincarnation?" she asked.

He gave her an odd look. "You mean like coming back in another life as a cat or a tree?"

"No. More like past lives. I feel so…different here. There's something about these places that we visit. Even the cottage. It's like I've been here before. I've never felt that way any other place."

It wasn't just her relationship with Riley or the fact that this place was the home of her ancestors. Nor was it her mother's connection with Ireland. No, she felt this bond deep inside her soul, as if it were part of her DNA.

She climbed up into one of the arches and stared out at the countryside. There was no place more beautiful. The thought of leaving Ireland made her heart ache and yet she knew this wasn't home.

"You look like some ancient high priestess," Riley said, "standing there with the wind blowing your skirt."

She smiled, then turned to face him. "I can understand why people believed in the power of this place," she said. "I can feel it all around me."

"It's all that Irish blood pumping through your veins," he murmured.

She'd refused to discuss their argument from the previous night. Nan still hadn't made a decision about what she was going to do. Though she wanted to know the truth, talking about her mother might be more upsetting than she anticipated. Since arriving in Ireland, her emotions had been unpredictable. What had begun as a simple quest to meet an old girlfriend of her mother's had turned into something so much more complicated.

"Give me your hand," Riley said, holding his out.

When she did, he carefully removed the ring he'd given her. "What're you doing?"

"What I should have done the first time I gave this to you. Come with me." He wrapped his hands around her waist as she jumped down, then he led her to the doorway blocked with iron bars.

The bars were just far enough apart for Riley to slip through and when he was on the other side, he reached for her. "Come on. Let's see where this goes."

She glanced over her shoulder. "No. They don't want us to go in there. That's why they put bars across the doorway."

"They didn't put them close enough together," he said. "So they must want us to slip through."

"What if we get caught?"

"By who?"

"Whom."

"By whom?" Riley said. "There's no one here. And I don't think we'd be breaking any laws. I promise, you won't regret it."

Reluctantly, she stepped through the gate and into a winding stairwell made entirely of stone. Some of the steps were crumbling but it was so solidly built that Nan didn't even hesitate before starting the climb. They came out on the top of a high wall, a perfect lookout to the countryside around them.

"Oh, look at this," Nan cried. "It's amazing."

"I told you," Riley said. He walked over to the wall and sat down on it, dangling his feet over the edge.

She joined him, leaving her legs on the safe side of the wall. Riley took her hand again. "I need to fix something," he said. "I want to do it right now." He put the ring on the end of her finger. "When you wear the heart pointing out on your right hand, it means you're looking for love. But when you turn the ring around, and the heart points at you, that means you're taken."

Nan stared down at her finger. She'd worn the ring for two days, believing it was just a pretty piece of jewelry. But suddenly, it meant something more. "I don't understand."

"I don't, either," Riley said. "I've been trying to figure this out since the moment we met. But something seems to be happening between us and I have a need to try to define it. So, this is as close as I can come for now. I want to be with you, Nan, and only with you."

"For how long?"

"I don't know. For as long as you want to be with me. But if it's longer than ten days, don't be afraid to tell me. You can stay, Nan. I want you to stay."

Nan looked up into his eyes and saw the truth in his words. And now that he'd said what she'd hoped to hear, Nan wasn't sure what to do. It had started as a wonderful vacation love affair that had a very clear beginning and end. But now, everything had changed. He'd offered her a choice and she wasn't sure whether she had the strength to make it.

"So, it's like we're going together?" she asked.

"Yes."

She giggled. "It seems a bit silly. I mean, we've already slept together and more than just once. I just assumed you wouldn't be doing the same with other women."

"That's not what I'm talking about," he said. "That's in the past. This is about the future."

Nan frowned, biting at her bottom lip as she considered his words. "I have to go home on Wednesday."

"No, you don't," Riley said. "You're an adult and you can do whatever you want. You can stay. For the rest of the summer. You can stay until Christmas or forever, if you choose to. You just have to make the choice."

"And what about you? What will you do if I choose to leave?"

"I'm not sure. I guess I won't really know until that happens."

She looked down at the ring. Tears welled up inside her and she fought them back. Was this what her mother had gone through, leaving the boy she'd loved? Had she even considered staying? Or was she certain that her destiny wasn't here in Ireland? Suddenly, Nan needed to know answers to all the questions she had. There was only one place to find them, only one man who could tell her.

"I do care about you," she murmured. "And I think it's easy for you to ask me to stay. You don't have anything to lose. You're not leaving anything behind."

"What are you leaving?" he asked. "The way I see it, you're all alone. Your parents are gone. You don't have any brothers or sisters."

"My life is there. A life I built for myself. Could you just give up everything here and move to the States?"

"I think I could. If it meant we might have a chance."

She shook her head, then took off the ring. "I can't do this," she said, holding the ring out for him to take. "This is all happening too fast."

"No," Riley said, pushing her hand away. "I want

you to keep it. Turn it the other way, I don't care." He cursed softly. "I shouldn't have said anything."

"It's all right," she said. "I'm not angry."

He drew a ragged breath, than pasted a smile on his face. "Why don't we just forget this conversation ever happened. We'll rewind."

"All right," Nan said. She put the ring back on her finger, this time with the heart pointing out. But it was impossible to erase the words he'd said. And though she'd heard him, Nan wasn't really sure what he'd meant. Was he making some kind of commitment to her?

Nan walked along the wall and stared down at the old graveyard. Ancient Celtic crosses marked the resting places of people who'd been forgotten generations ago. These people had loved and laughed and dreamed about the future.

She drew in a sharp breath. Maybe they were trying to tell her something from beyond the grave. Maybe she needed to take a chance, to live her life by her heart and not her head. Life was too short for doubts and hesitation.

She had three more nights to decide, three more nights spent in his arms. Nan made a silent promise to herself. When it came time to make that decision, she wouldn't think. She'd just allow herself to feel. If she did that, everything would turn out right.

NAN DECIDED TO SPEND Monday on her own. Though Riley hadn't been happy with the decision, she wanted to put a bit of space between them after his "proposal" at the abbey. She was finding it more and more difficult to think logically and rationally when she was around him. He'd asked her to stay and Nan had almost convinced herself that she could.

He'd made it quite clear how he felt and what he wanted, yet Nan wasn't sure she could even make such a momentous decision. But she had made a step in the right direction. She'd decided that it was time to pay a visit to Carey Findley. She'd promised to be back in time for dinner, telling him they'd make a picnic and walk down to the bluffs to watch the sun set.

The drive to Kealkill had been simple given the map she'd found in the car. But as she'd neared the village, Nan had noticed signs for a castle and a stone circle, so she'd deliberately taken a detour, needing more time to work up her courage.

She stood in the center of the old stone circle, located in another farmer's field just outside Kealkill. Yes, she was wasting time, loitering at a spot where pagans had danced and paid homage to their gods. With a soft sigh, she walked around the small circle, her palm dragging across the weathered stones.

If her mother's story was as she suspected, what Carey Findley knew could change everything. She had become her mother, coming to this magical place and fallen in love with a handsome Irishman. They had a common experience and everything she was feeling, her mother had felt as well. But she could make the choice to stay, to believe in this place and in the love she'd found.

Nan stood in the center of the circle again, tipping

her face up to the noonday sun. She threw her hands out and closed her eyes. An odd feeling washed over her and suddenly, she felt as if she wasn't alone.

A dog barked and Nan spun around to see a little black terrier running toward her. She froze, waiting for the dog to chomp into her leg. But, instead, he put his paws on her knee and wagged his tail.

"Don't you worry, lass. He doesn't bite. Come on, Georgie. Leave the lady alone."

The dog sniffed at her feet and Nan reached down and gave him a pet. The little dog licked her hand before taking off again.

An elderly man carrying a long walking stick peeked around the corner of the stone, smiling warmly. "Sorry. He's not afraid of strangers, that one."

"It's all right," Nan said. "He just startled me for a second."

"So, what are you doin' out here all alone? Communing with the Druid spirits?"

"Something like that," she said with a soft laugh. "It's a magical place."

"That it is," the man said. "That it is. I walk out here almost every day. Now and then, I catch sight of a faerie or two, though they're easier to see at twilight."

"I would love to see a faerie before I leave," she said.

"You're from America?"

Nan nodded. "Just visiting. I'm staying in Ballykirk."

"I know it well," he said. "I used to have a farm near there."

Nan held out her hand. "I'm Nan. Nan Galvin."

He reached to take her hand, then froze at the sound

of her name. His hand trembled slightly. "Tiernan Galvin?"

"Yes," she said. "How did you—" An odd feeling washed over her again and she felt suddenly calm. "And you're Carey, aren't you? Carey Findley."

"Yes. I am."

She shook her head, wondering at the mystical forces that had brought them together in his spot. It wasn't just coincidence. She'd been drawn to this place for a reason. They were meant to meet. "This is so strange. A little bit spooky. I've read all your letters. I feel like I know you."

"I got a call from your friend Riley Quinn. I was wondering if you'd stop to see me. I've been leaving a note on my door each day when I go out."

"I wasn't sure I'd come," she said. "But I guess I didn't have to make the decision after all."

Nan scrambled for a way to begin. She thought she'd have more time to explain why she'd come and what she wanted. But here he was, watching her with twinkling eyes and a bright smile.

"Maybe we should sit down," she said. Nan pointed to a boulder sitting outside the stone circle. Carey followed her, taking a spot beside her.

She opened her mouth, then snapped it shut. "I don't know where to begin."

"Then allow me," he said. "I wondered if you'd ever come. After your mother stopped writing, I thought maybe she'd decided she wasn't going to ever tell you about Tiernan."

"No," Nan said, shaking her head. "She stopped writing because she died."

His expression fell and she saw his eyes grow watery with tears. "I thought that might have been it," he said. "She mentioned in some of her last letters that she was ill, but she didn't give me any details."

"You knew my mother?"

"I did," he said. "She stayed at our farm with some of her friends. We used to let out a few of the extra bedrooms to students traveling around Ireland. Oh, she was a lively young woman, always laughing and teasing. She couldn't keep still."

"And your son? What was he like?"

"Handsome. Charming. Probably too charming for his own good, that one. All the girls loved him, but your mother, she was the one who captured his heart. When she left, he was so sad and angry."

"I'm sorry about what happened to him," Nan said.

Carey nodded, his face etched with grief. "It was a bad time. And my wife, she never really recovered. He was our only child and she grieved for him until the day she died."

"Did they love each other? Tiernan and my mother?"

He folded his hands over his walking stick. "Oh, yes. I do think so. They were both so young, but they were happy together. When we got the news, it was difficult for Tiernan. My son wasn't ready to be a father and Laura had no support over here, so she didn't—"

"I don't understand," Nan said. "You said Tiernan was going to be a father. Did he get another girl pregnant? Is that why my mother left?"

The old man took a long breath then shook his head wearily. "You don't know. You haven't figured it out, have you?"

Nan pressed her hand to her chest. Had her heart stopped beating? Why couldn't she breathe? "The baby was me," she murmured. "It was me?"

"I'm sorry. I thought that's why you'd come. That's why I'd written to your mother for all those years. I wanted news of my granddaughter. You're my granddaughter, Tiernan."

Nan stood and walked over to one of the tall stones, pressing her hands against it as she tried to breathe again. Now, everything made perfect sense. Somewhere, deep inside her, she thought this might be it, but she'd refused to consider it.

"She was pregnant when she left?"

Carey shook his head. "When your mother got home, she found out she was pregnant. She knew Tiernan was the father and she wrote him a letter to tell him. He threw the letter in the rubbish and I found it and read it. I wrote back to her, begging her to come and live with us, determined to make Tiernan stand by her. But by that time, she'd already married your father."

"But then Tiernan died," Nan murmured.

"No one knew about you, outside of our family. But it changed him. He became more reckless, more headstrong. I think, in the end, he realized how much he loved Laura and what a mistake he'd made. But, by then, it was too late."

"You lost your grandchild and then your child."

"It killed my wife. After Tiernan's accident, she

couldn't bring herself to look at your mother's letters. She was even afraid to look at your photos for fear she might love you and that you might resemble Tiernan—which you do, by the way. Living so far away from you was too much for her to bear."

"I read your letters," Nan said. "They're what brought me here. What if I'd never found them? What if my father had thrown them away? I never would have known."

"I still have the letters she sent me. And all the photos she sent. And she left a sketchbook that I found in Tiernan's room after he died. I think you should have them."

"I'd love to see them," Nan said.

Carey stood up and whistled for his dog. "Come along, then. I live just down the lane. We'll walk and chat on the way."

Nan got up, her knees wobbly and her emotions barely in check, and they started toward the road. Carey peppered her with questions about her life, from her very first memories of her childhood to what she'd been doing a week ago. She answered him numbly, her body and mind on autopilot.

She wanted to sit down in the middle of the road and just take a moment. Everything seemed to be moving so fast, she hadn't had time to react. She felt like crying and laughing at the same time.

How hard had it been for her father? He must have known, yet he kept the secret all these years, raising the child of another man. And what about her mother, walking away from the boy she loved and stepping into a marriage of convenience, merely to give her daughter a name? Her entire life had been one big charade.

As Carey had said, his cottage was only a quarter mile down the road from the stone circle. It was a tidy little home, much like the Quinn cottage, whitewashed but with a slate roof and pretty blue front door. They walked through the front garden and he held the door open for her, Georgie scampering in beneath her feet.

"I'll just put on the water for a pot of tea," he said. He pointed to the comfortable parlor. "Sit down and take a rest. I know this is a lot to comprehend in a very short time."

Dazed, Nan walked into the cozy room then noticed the framed photos sitting on a shelf between the windows. She crossed to examine them more closely, then realized many of them were of her as a child. She drew a ragged breath and tears flooded her eyes.

This man was her grandfather. She wasn't alone anymore. She had family. Nan picked up a photo of a handsome boy with dark hair and devilish eyes. And this was her father. "Tiernan," she murmured, running her fingers over his image, tears streaming down her cheeks.

Carey reappeared, clutching a large black book in his arms. Wiping the tears away with her sleeve, Nan sat down and took the book from his outstretched hands. She recognized what it was immediately. Her father had given her three or four of her mother's old sketchbooks, filled with drawings of Nan and various places around their neighborhood. But these drawings would be from before Nan even existed.

"Open it," Carey said. "I think she left it with Tiernan as a kind of memory of the time they spent together. When I moved from the farm, I found it in his closet and I kept it. I always hoped that one day, I'd get to meet you and I could give it back."

She hugged it to her chest. "Thank you. I—I think I'll look at it later."

"Well, I'd expect this has all come as quite a shock to you."

Nan nodded. "I'm not sure what to say. This morning, I didn't have a family and now I do."

"When are you planning to return home?"

"I have a flight back in a few days," she said. "On Wednesday."

"If you have a mind to write a letter now and then, I would promise to write back. And I hope we could exchange some photos." He hurried across to the shelf and took the photo of Tiernan down. "You should take this. You need a photo of him."

She looked at Carey, at the hope that was in his eyes. He'd never even known her, yet she could tell he didn't want her to leave. Maybe, he even loved her like every grandfather loved his granddaughter. She tried to imagine him, opening her mother's letters, staring at the photos, trying to know the girl she was. "Thank you," she murmured.

"And if you ever come back to Ireland, you must promise to visit."

Nan nodded. "Yes. I promise." She paused. "Do you really think they were in love?"

"Oh, yes. I know they were," he said. "If you'd have seen them together, you'd have known it, too. But I don't believe your mother was ready to give up her life in America to marry an Irish boy she barely knew. She made the right decision. My son wasn't ready to be a husband or a father. Ireland would have been an unhappy place for both of you."

Nan quickly stood. This was too much to take in all at once. "I—I should go. But—but I'll come back. Tomorrow."

"Yes," he said. "Tomorrow. I'll have your mother's letters for you. Maybe you'd like to come for a late breakfast? Or lunch?"

"Yes," Nan said. "Breakfast would be nice." She hurried to the door, then turned around. "Thank you."

He smiled. "No, thank you. You've made an old man very happy."

Nan slipped outside, then hurried down the front walk to the road. She started out at a brisk walk, but in the end, she ran, the sketchbook and photo pressed against her chest. When she reached her car, Nan leaned against the bumper and drew a deep breath.

Everything had changed. She had another grandfather, and another father. A life here in Ireland that she'd never had a chance to live. Nan opened the car door and slipped behind the wheel, carefully placing the book and photo on the passenger seat.

She'd go home, to the cottage and to Riley, to a place she felt safe. And she'd tell him everything she'd learned. He'd know what to make of it.

RILEY PACED BACK and forth in front of the hearth. It was nearly six and Nan had promised to be back before dinner. He glanced at his watch again. He should have sent his mobile with her and insisted that she call if she was going to be late. She could have had car trouble along the way. He should have demanded that she take his car instead of the Fiat.

"Idiot," he muttered to himself. "I'm a feckin' idiot."

He walked back to the kitchen and checked on the dinner he'd prepared. The shepherd's pie was sitting on top of the cooker, stone cold. And the bread he'd tossed in the oven to warm was so dry it was hard as a rock.

Riley grabbed the bottle of wine and removed the cork. Maybe getting pissed would make the time pass faster. He wasn't going to worry until dark. She could have gotten lost or just wrapped up in some interesting spot she found.

He didn't bother with a glass and drank the wine directly out of the bottle. The sound of a car on the road caught his attention and Riley strode to the front door and pulled it open.

To his relief, the Fiat appeared from below the rise and sputtered to a stop at the front gate. He cursed softly, but continued to stand in the doorway in an attempt to cool his temper. He wanted to demand an explanation but the moment she stepped inside the gate, he strode up the walk and pulled her into his arms.

His mouth came down on hers in a desperate kiss. Was she all right? Had anything changed? She looked nervous and upset and her eyes were red. Riley ran his fingers through her hair, then drew back. "I was worried. Is everything all right?"

"I—I'm sorry I'm late."

He grinned and gave her a hug. "You should be. Dinner is ruined. But then, it probably wasn't much good to start with."

"You made dinner?" A wide smile broke across her pretty features. "That's sweet."

"Well, I didn't exactly make it myself. It came frozen and I put it in the oven. Shepherd's pie. And bread."

"Yum," she said. Sighing softly, she wrapped her arms around his waist and rested her head on his chest. "I went to see him today."

Riley stepped back and hooked her chin with his thumb, forcing her gaze to meet his. "Carey Findley?"

She nodded, then looked up into his gaze. "He's my grandfather."

"What?"

"I'm Tiernan's daughter. That's why I have his name. After my mother left Ireland, she found out she was pregnant with me. She wrote to him and he didn't want anything to do with me, so she married my father." Emotion clogged her throat and tears tumbled from her eyes. Wrapped in the curve of his arm, Nan slowly walked into the cottage. He drew her along to the sofa and they sat, Riley wiping the tears from her cheeks with his fingers.

"Oh, I'm sorry. I never even imagined that this was possible. Did you?"

"Maybe. It made so much sense once I knew. Everything fell into place." She forced a smile and looked at him through watery eyes. "He's so nice, Riley. He had all these pictures of me up in his parlor. Photos my mother sent him from when I was little. And he gave me her sketchbook and a photo of Tier—My father. Biological father." She glanced over her shoulder. "I left them in the car. Let me go get them."

"No," he said. "I don't want to let you go just yet."

She sank against him. "I never really had grandparents. Not the kind that everyone has. My mother was estranged from her parents and I can see why now. And my father's parents died before I was born. But Carey is like one of those sweet, smiling grandfathers that you see in the movies."

"Then you're happy you went?"

She nodded. "I'm happy I know the truth. It still hasn't completely sunk in, but I think I'll be all right."

"I missed you," he murmured, cupping her face in his palms and kissing her.

Nan giggled, then brushed aside a tear. "You did?"

"More that you can imagine," he said with a low growl.

"Oh, no," Nan said. "Don't look at me like that."

"Like what?"

"Like you want to drag me off to bed. I know that look."

"You don't," Riley insisted. "I'll get you a glass of wine, we'll take a blanket up on the hill and we'll relax. Wait right here."

Riley pulled a quilt from the chest in the second bedroom, then grabbed two glasses. The wine was still sitting on the table by the door. When he got back outside, she was waiting by the gate, a large black book in her arms.

They walked up the rise behind the house to a spot

in front of a drystone wall. Wildflowers swayed in the evening breeze, perfuming the air around them. Nan spread the quilt out and sat down, then took the glasses from him.

"Tell me everything," Riley said. "Did you spend the entire day with him?"

"No," she said. "When I left, I wasn't even sure that I was going to stop at his place. First, I went to see Carriganass Castle and then I went to a stone circle. And I was thinking of going to see him and then this man walked up with a little black dog and it was him."

"What?"

"Right there. At the stone circle. He was there, as if I conjured him up out of thin air."

"That's odd. Spooky."

"I know," Nan said. "That's exactly what I said. Even if I had decided I didn't want to meet him, we would have met. I went to his house and we talked for a little bit, but then I got overwhelmed and I had to leave. I promised I'd come back tomorrow." She took his hand, weaving her fingers through his. "You'll come with me, won't you?"

"Sure." Riley poured her a glass of wine and handed it to her, then filled a glass for himself. "So, why don't we have a toast?"

"To what?" Nan asked.

"To your newfound family. And to your citizenship," he said. "You are now a citizen of the Republic of Ireland."

Nan stared at him in disbelief. "No, I'm not."

"Yes, you are. If either of your parents are Irish citizens, then you automatically are. That's the way it works here. You'll probably have to do a few things to make it official, but that shouldn't be too difficult."

Nan stared at him for a long time, then finally shook her head. "I suddenly feel very Irish. I'm going to start talking with a brogue."

"Well, Tiernan Galvin," he began in a deep Irish accent, "let me teach you a few important things. You already know the proper use of 'feck' and its various forms. 'Bloody' can be used in almost any situation. But then there's 'bollocks.'"

"Bollocks," she repeated.

"No. You have to say it with more attitude. Bollocks!"

"Bollocks!" Nan said, bursting into giggles. "What does it mean?"

"Stupid. A mess. A hames. Ruined. Destroyed. It's just a term that applies to anything that's royally fecked up. It also means testicles."

"I can't say that!"

"Shag," he said. "That means anything that has to do with sex."

"I know that one," she said. "But what's a culchie? Kellan called you that."

"Someone who lives in the country. Also known as a bogger or a bog-trotter. Unlike Kellan, who is a jackeen. He lives in Dublin."

"I have so much to learn," she said.

"You don't even know the half of it," Riley said. He grabbed her glass and set it in the grass, then pulled her beneath him on the blanket. "I'll teach you the rest."

"Are we going to shag now?" she asked, barely able to contain her laughter.

"No. Not until you stop giggling."

"If we were in the States we'd be doing the horizontal mambo. Or making whoopee. Or boinking. My co-worker calls it baking cookies."

"Well, that's good to know. If I'm ever in the States, I'll know what to say when soliciting sex."

"If you're ever in the States, you'll get arrested for doing that. And I wouldn't come and bail you out."

"You're the only one I want," Riley murmured. He kissed her softly, then covered her mouth with his. His tongue tangled with hers and he moaned softly, already growing hard. Hell, it didn't take much. A little talk, a few kisses, and he was lost.

They kissed for a long time, Riley enjoying the taste of her mouth and the feel of her body beneath his touch. But he didn't want to go any further. He'd leave that for later, when they were naked in her bed. Instead, he curled up beside her, his leg thrown over her thighs, his chin tucked into her shoulder.

"I missed you today," he murmured. "I didn't know what to do with myself."

"What did you do before I got here?"

"I don't even remember. But it must not have been very interesting."

"What will you do after I leave?"

"I don't know. I don't even want to think about that. I'll probably hang out at the airport hoping you'll just decide to come back some day."

"That's pretty pathetic," she whispered, turning to look at him.

"I know. But now, you have a reason to come back. Your grandfather is here. I'm not so sad anymore."

"Mmm-hmm. I don't want you to be sad." She ran her hands through his hair, then kissed his forehead. "I'm sure you'll be fine."

He couldn't bring himself to agree with her. In truth, he knew for a fact that, if today were any example, he'd spend the first month drunk and the second pissed off at the world. Maybe, by the third month, he'd be tolerable, but just barely. "Sure," Riley said. "I'll be grand."

8

Nan stood at the gate to the old cemetery, running her hand over the ornate ironwork. She was always amazed at how, everywhere she looked, there was something beautiful to see. Even the lichen-covered Celtic crosses, their detail worn away by time, were like little monuments to the past.

She'd passed the cemetery several times on her way in and out of town and had always wanted to take a closer look. It was only now that she realized the importance of the place. Her father, Tiernan Findley, had been buried here. This was probably her last chance to visit him before she left.

The past few days had been an emotional roller coaster, full of tears and confusion, questions and doubts. But she'd survived it all, only a little bruised. And it had kept her mind off the real sadness—saying goodbye to Riley and Ireland.

They'd driven back to Kealkill and spent the morning with her grandfather, sharing a traditional Irish breakfast in Carey's garden. They'd talked about her mother and she'd answered all the questions he hadn't asked the day before. And when it was time to leave, Nan had felt her emotions well up inside of her, so quickly that she could barely say goodbye.

Standing in the cemetery now, she swallowed the lump in her throat. She'd see him again. In truth, her grandfather gave her the perfect excuse to come back to Ireland. Glancing both ways, Nan stepped through the graveyard gate.

A chilly breeze swirled around her, causing a shiver to run through her body and she pulled her sweater more tightly around her. From a tree on the other side of the wall, a flock of jackdaws cawed. An eerie feeling came over her and Nan nearly turned back, then decided she was being silly. She'd weathered all the other emotional storms that had come her way. What was she afraid of now?

As she began to wander among the stones, she read the names and the dates of death. Some of them were recent, one stone marking a grave that was still covered with dirt. "Aina M. Garrity," she read from the stone. "Eighty-seven years old. A long life." She'd died just a month before.

Nan moved to the older section of the cemetery. There were stones from the time of the famine, single stones marking large plots for multiple family members. The children's stones broke her heart. They'd died from scarlet fever or typhus or any of the simple illnesses that were so easily cured today.

The Quinn family plot stood near the edge of the cemetery. "Rory Quinn," she read. "Beloved wife,

Brenna Rooney Quinn." How were these people related to Riley? "Jack Quinn. Siobhan Quinn." Siobhan had lived for eleven years without her husband beside her. Had she been lonely?

She found Tiernan's grave nearby, the newer stone gleaming in the sun. Squatting down, she brushed away the grass to read the inscription. "Tiernan Findlay, born June 13, 1960. Died November 3, 1984." The next words were in Gaelic. *Go gcasaimid ar a chéile arís.*

The sound of a dog barking caught her attention and Nan stood up to see Riley's brother, Danny, striding briskly down the road. Two black-and-white dogs raced ahead of him. He whistled for them and they came running back then sat at the gate and peered inside at her.

When Danny noticed her, he slowed his pace. "Keep an eye out," he teased. "Aina Garrity has been haunting this place for the last month."

Nan frowned. "The lady that died?"

He grinned and stopped at the gate. "She's hanging about, waiting for the next funeral."

"But she's dead."

"Her ghost can't leave until someone else is buried."

Nan slowly walked toward the gate, that same eerie feeling coming over her. Now she was spooked. Had Aina Garrity been watching her? Had the dead woman's ghost been up in the trees with the crows?

"It's a beautiful cemetery," Nan said. "I was just admiring the stones."

He grinned, reaching down to pat one of his dogs. "They are beautiful," he said. "We Irish do death so well."

"Can you read Gaelic? There's an inscription on a stone. I'd like to know what it means."

He stepped through the gate and followed her to Tiernan's grave, the dogs scampering around his feet. Danny stood in front of the gravestone and stared at it, then glanced over at Nan. "Riley told us about your news."

She nodded. "Do you know what it means?"

"Until we meet again."

She drew a deep breath, then smiled. "That's nice. I like that."

"Are you through here? I was just walking into town. I have to open the pub for lunch."

Nan nodded. "I told Riley I'd meet him there." She took one last look at the gravestone, committing it to memory, then turned for the gate.

Danny held it open for her and she smiled and pointed to the beautiful work. "Did you do this? Riley said you're a blacksmith."

"I did," Danny said. "It was one of the first projects I did. My ma said it would help my way into heaven."

He closed the gate behind her and they strolled down the road side by side, the dogs bounding ahead of them both. "What did you mean about Aina Garrity?"

"I was just teasing. Silly Irish superstition," he said.

"Tell me," Nan said.

"Oh, where should I start? When someone dies, their ghost is required to stay at the churchyard and tend to the dead until the next corpse comes along. They're supposed to carry water to Purgatory for the folks down there. When two people are buried on the same day, the families race to the cemetery to bury their loved one first so they get the express train to heaven."

She giggled. "So Aina is stuck until another ghost shows up."

Danny nodded. "That's not the worst of it. Some of the older folks believe that a dead hand is a cure to all sickness."

"Ew," Nan said. "You have to eat a dead hand?"

"No," Danny cried, shaking his head. "We're not that macabre. If you're ill, you just have to be touched by a dead hand. So all the sick relatives come to the wake so they can be touched by the dearly departed's hand."

Nan shuddered. "I felt like I was being watched in the churchyard."

"If a ghost or an evil spirit chases you, they can't follow you across water. So find a stream and jump over it."

"Good to know," Nan said with a laugh.

"Don't worry. Aina can't leave the cemetery, so you're safe."

"I saw some Quinns there."

"My grandparents are buried there. Rory and Brenna Quinn. And Rory's parents, Jack and Siobhan. Jack was shot during the Irish rebellion and Siobhan also worked for the cause. That was his fishing boat that you and Riley took to Bantry. And Rory was a pilot for the RAF during the second world war. The Quinns have always lived large."

"Riley said you were an artist. Can I see your work?"

He grinned. "Sure. I have some things in my workshop. We can stop on our way to the pub if you'd like."

"I would," Nan said.

They strolled along in the warm noonday sun, watching the dogs run ahead of them. Danny was as charming as Riley, amusing her with a complete education of Irish superstition. By the time they reached his workshop, she could only wonder how the Quinn boys had remained single for as long as they had.

She followed Danny around the back of cottage to what looked like a small barn. He pulled a large door open and Nan stepped into the dimly lit interior. Ornate ironwork hung from the old timber beams and along one wall, large swaths of canvas hid his sculptures. Danny pulled them off one by one, revealing wildly imaginative work. Nan stared in awe at his sculptures.

"This is incredible," she murmured, walking from piece to piece.

"This is what I do in my spare time," he said.

She moved to a small wooden case, filled with tiny carvings of animals and insects. "What are these?"

"I did those when I was a kid. That's how I got my start, in bath soap and driftwood." He reached up to a shelf that hung from the stone wall. "Here. I have something for you."

He handed her an ornate Celtic cross made from cast iron. The detailing on it was incredible and she gazed at it in awe. "That came from my religious phase," he said with a wry smile. "I did a whole series of them. This is the only one left."

"I—I can't take this," she said.

"Sure you can," Danny said. "It will ward off evil

spirits and it works as a deterrent to pickpockets and highwaymen."

"Have you ever shown your work at a gallery?" she asked.

"I have a show every few years in Dublin at a gallery there. But I don't have much time for my art. I spend most of my days making practical things like gates and andirons. They pay the bills."

Nan stood in front of a sculpture of a giant soaring bird, its wings reaching out like arms to the sky. "I don't know a lot about art, but I know this is good. It makes me feel something."

"There's one just like it in Dublin. It was a commission from the mayor's arts council."

He spent the next half hour showing her all of his pieces, explaining each one and answering all her questions. Nan was surprised at how easy it was to talk to Riley's brother. He was just like…family.

He seemed genuinely interested in her opinions and appreciated her comments about her favorite pieces. From the start, with Riley, it had been all about the attraction between them, so powerful and intense. But Danny seemed like a good friend, only interested in chatting with her.

When they'd finished the impromptu show, Nan watched as he covered all his sculptures, wondering what it would be like to become a part of this family. She was all alone in the world now, except for her Irish grandfather.

She could only guess at why her mother's parents never been a part of her life. Maybe they'd never wanted her mother to have an illegitimate child. Or maybe they disapproved of her marrying an older man. Certainly, an unexpected pregnancy would come as a shock to any parent, especially when the father of the baby wanted nothing to do with the mother. But Laura Daley had decided to do what she needed to do to make a life for her daughter.

Maybe she had still loved Tiernan. Maybe she died with his image in her mind. It was a romantic notion that they were finally together. Was that what the inscription had meant? Until they meet again.

Or perhaps his betrayal had ended any feelings she'd ever had. But one thing was certain. She had wanted the baby growing inside her and she'd probably defied her parents in making that choice.

"So, Riley tells me you'll be leaving us soon," Danny said as they continued their walk into Ballykirk.

"I go home tomorrow," Nan said. "I don't want to leave. I haven't seen half of what I came here to see. I had all these carefully laid plans and they all fell apart."

"Plans have a way of doing that now, don't they," he said with a wry smile. "Maybe your plans to go home should suffer the same consequences."

"I have a job I have to get back to," she said.

"Is it something you love?" he asked.

She opened her mouth to reply, but then realized that her automatic affirmation wasn't really what she felt. Was she as passionate about her work as Danny was? He mentioned that he had to sculpt, that he had no other choice in the matter. But Nan couldn't work up such strong feelings for her own career.

Yes, liked what she did, but it wasn't important work. Not like Riley's music and Danny's art. If Nan didn't do her work, they'd find someone else who would. She was easily replaced.

"Yes," she lied. "I really do love it."

"Well, then, it won't be so difficult to leave Ireland, I'd expect."

When they reached the pub, Danny opened the front door and they walked inside the quiet interior. Riley was standing behind the bar, scribbling something on a pad of paper. He looked up as they came in, glancing between them both at first, his expression unreadable.

"I met Nan on the road into town," Danny explained.

"He took me to see his studio," Nan added, wondering at the chilly look Riley gave Danny. "I guess we lost track of time."

Riley pointed at the clock. "Yeah, well, you're late, little brother."

"Jaysus, Riley, what's fifteen minutes?"

"Twenty," Riley said. "And considering I only have today left with Nan, it's more than I'm willing to give up to you." He tossed his apron at Danny, then circled the bar and grabbed Nan's hand. He drew her toward the door. "Come on, let's get the hell out of here."

"Thanks for the tour, Danny," she called, waving at him as she hurried out the door. "If I don't see you again, it was nice meeting you."

When they got outside, Nan pulled her hand from his and stopped, refusing to take another step. "That was rude."

"He's my brother. I'm allowed."

"Why are you such a grump? We just walked into town together. He was nice to me and showed me his work."

"That usually does the trick with the girls here in town," Riley said.

She gasped, stunned that he'd think there was something going on between her and his brother. "Wow, you did get up on the wrong side of the bed this morning."

He cursed softly, then ran his fingers through his hair. "Right. Well, how the hell am I supposed to feel? It's like time is slipping through my fingers and I can't do anything to stop it, Nan. You're going home tomorrow and we may never see each other again and you don't seem to give a shite."

Nan stared at him. What was this all about? He'd never spoken to her like that and she could see anger in his eyes. She sighed, then turned and walked up the street toward the cottage.

"Oh, that's fine now," Riley shouted. "Just walk away. We can't even have a disagreement?"

Nan turned to face him, walking backward. "You're making an arse of yourself," she shouted. "And I don't think I like you anymore."

RILEY CURSED AGAIN, this time out loud. She was absolutely right. He was acting like a horse's arse, but he couldn't seem to help himself. Just the thought of her getting on a plane and going back to the States was enough to make him crazy with frustration.

No doubt, she'd go back to the cottage and pout for a bit, then he'd come crawling back with an apology for being a stupid prick. And they'd tumble into bed and everything would be set right again. But he didn't want to waste even that much time staying angry.

He ran after her and caught up in a matter of seconds. "All right. I'm sorry. I can't help that I want to spend every waking minute with you as well as all the minutes that we're asleep. And I know you were just being nice to Danny and I shouldn't fault you for that."

"He happens to be a very nice guy. Unlike you."

"I am a nice guy under ordinary circumstances," he said. "But this isn't really something I'm accustomed to, so you'll have to give me a break."

"Was there an apology in there?" Nan asked. "Because I didn't hear it."

"I'm sorry," he said, taking her hand and drawing it to his lips. "Very sorry. Will you forgive me?"

She sent him a sideways glance, then rolled her eyes. "There was nothing to be jealous of," she said. "You were so nasty to your brother. You should treat him better. And appreciate that you even have a brother. I don't have any siblings, but if I did, I would love them every day."

"You're right," Riley said. "And I promise to apologize to Danny when I see him the next time. Now, would you like me to beg for your forgiveness or can I just kiss you now and forget any of this happened."

"You can kiss me later," she said. "I want to make myself some lunch and then start packing."

They walked together out of town, both of them silent, Riley waiting for her to smile at him. "So, what did you and Danny talk about?"

Nan shrugged. "Mostly his work," she said. "He was walking his dogs and passed by the cemetery. I was there, looking at the gravestones. I found my father's. Danny translated the inscription for me. It said, 'until we meet again.'" She met his gaze. "Isn't that a nice sentiment. It sounds so hopeful."

"It's sad," he said. "And it doesn't always happen. Meeting again. Sometimes people part and that's the end of it. Look at your mother and Tiernan."

"I'd like to think they have met again. And maybe, their spirits are now able to continue on with what they began all those years ago."

"Or maybe we're the ones who are doing that for them. Did you ever think of that? Maybe it's us who shouldn't be saying those words."

"I'm hungry," she said, deftly changing the subject.

He'd been pushing her at every opportunity, trying to force her to see how difficult it would be to leave. But Nan was stubbornly sticking to her plans, unable to commit to a life in Ireland with him.

Riley pointed to the small bakery just down the street. "They make the best sausage rolls. I'll buy you lunch."

They walked inside the bakery and, in addition to the sausage rolls, Riley purchased a small apple tart to share and two Cokes. They walked back outside and sat down at one of the tables in front of the bakery.

"You look very pretty this morning," he said, handing her the Coke.

"Oh, and flattery won't get you anywhere," she said.

"What will get me somewhere?" he inquired.

She took a bite of the sausage roll and considered his question. "Are you passionate about your job?"

"I don't really have a job," he said.

"No, I mean your music. You're a singer. That's how you make money, right?"

"Not a lot of money, but, yes, I suppose that's right."

"Could you ever imagine yourself doing something else. Other than singing?"

"Sure. I expect I won't be flogging my guts out in the pubs until I'm eighty. I'll have to quit sooner or later."

"No, I don't think you understand what I'm saying." Nan frowned as she searched for a way to ask her question. He gave her hand a squeeze, wondering what had so consumed her thoughts. "Are you passionate about your singing? Would you be less of a person if you didn't do it?"

He thought about it for a long moment. In truth, he'd been thinking about that very question ever since Nan arrived. Could he walk away from performing and not miss it at all? Could he be happy working at something else merely to provide a decent living for a wife and family? Or were Riley the singer and Riley the man inseparable?

"I think I'm always going to have to perform," he said, the truth of his feelings bubbling to the surface. "I like how it makes me feel. It might not always bring financial rewards, but who knows. With the new CD, something might change. What about you?"

"I'm good at what I do, and I like that. People think I do a good job and I'm a valuable employee. But I'm beginning to think that maybe I've just been so comfortable at the library I never considered doing anything else."

Riley was stunned by her confession. It was the first indication she'd given that she might be open to a change in her life. If she wasn't that invested in her career, then maybe she'd consider leaving it behind.

Riley fought the urge to push the issue. He wasn't going to spend her last day in Ireland trying to convince her to stay. He was going to enjoy her company and make love to her one last time and then he was going to let her go.

He knew exactly how he felt, but Riley was still unsure about Nan's feelings. Every instinct told him there was a deep affection between them, but did she consider it the beginning of love or the end of an infatuation? He wanted to ask her, but at the same time, he was afraid of her answer.

"So, what's the plan for your last day in Ireland?"

"I don't know," Nan said. "There are so many things left on my list. But I think I've had enough of sightseeing. I think I want to find a pretty spot and just sit."

"Would you mind if I sat with you?" Riley asked.

"I think that would be nice. Why don't you take me to the prettiest spot around Ballykirk."

"I know the exact spot," Riley said. "But we have to stop at the cottage first and get a few things. A blanket. Something to eat and drink. And sturdy shoes for you."

"Where are we going?" she asked.

Riley wrapped his arm around her shoulders and pulled her close. "To one of my secret places. No one else knows about it."

"Really?"

"No," he said. "My brothers know about it, and probably a lot of other people. But I like to pretend that it is all mine."

They hiked back up to the cottage and Riley gathered up the makings of a picnic, then threw a blanket over his shoulder. Nan put on a pair of trainers and then waited for him at the front door.

"I'm excited," she said.

"Don't get too excited. I may have oversold this place." He picked up her straw hat from the table and set it on top of her head. "Put on some jeans and you might need a heavier cardie."

She returned from the bedroom with her jacket and tied the arms around her waist. "Am I ready now?"

He grinned, the dropped a kiss on her lips. "Before we leave, I need to swear you to an oath of secrecy. You are venturing into a place that is known to only the Quinns—me, my brother Kellan and my brother Danny. And if they knew I was showing you this, they'd probably be forced to do something rash."

She seemed amused by his teasing. Nan raised her hand. "I swear, I will reveal nothing of what I see today."

"Good. Then we're ready to go."

THE HIKE DOWN the rocky cliff to the sea was frightening at times, but Riley moved slowly, pointing out the places that she needed to navigate through the boulders. Nan had wondered at the possibility of reaching the water when they first stood on the top edge, but now, just ten feet from the coastline, she glanced back up to see how far they'd come.

Riley jumped down onto the sand, then held his hand out to her. "We're here," he said.

He clasped her waist and set her on her feet. They were inside a small cove on the bay, somewhere beyond Ballykirk harbor. It was a perfectly private spot, invisible from the top of the cliff and from the surrounding area. The only way to be seen was from a boat in the bay.

Nan smiled. The water from the bay lapped against the narrow strip of sand. "It's a beach," she said. "Can we swim?"

"The water is a bit chilly this time of year, but yes, my brothers and I used to swim here all the time." He laid the blanket out on the sand, then kicked off his shoes. "We used to call it Smuggler's Cove. There's a cave over there in the cliff side and we thought it was the perfect place for smugglers to hide."

"It's beautiful," she said.

"We have to make sure we leave by three," he said.

"Why?"

"Because the tide will come into the bay and this beach will be gone." He patted the blanket beside him. "Come here. I have an overwhelming need to kiss you."

Nan sat down next to him and he dragged her on top of him, his fingers furrowing through her hair. "Ten days isn't long enough," he murmured. "I'm just getting used to having you here and now you have to go away."

Nan looked down into his eyes. She didn't want to

think about tomorrow. Pressing her finger over his lips, she shook her head. "We're here now. And I'm not going anywhere, at least not until the tide comes in."

She straddled his hips, then slipped out of her sweater. Her shirt followed, leaving her only in her bra. Riley's gaze raked her body as he cupped her breast in his palm. Nan closed her eyes and tipped her face up to the sun. "This is exactly how I wanted to spend my last day here."

She looked so beautiful, Riley mused. A memory flickered in his mind and searched for it. "Have you ever had a sexual fantasy?" Riley asked.

Nan glanced down at him, a tiny frown furrowing her brow. "Why do you ask?"

"Because I'm in the early stage of one right now," he replied. Riley chuckled softly. "When I was a teenager, I'd come down here and I'd think about what I'd do if I found a selkie on the beach. I'd try to picture what she'd look like and you're what I used to picture."

"No," she murmured.

"Yes," he said. "I used to always like women with long hair, but my selkie always had short dark hair. Just like yours."

"Maybe you knew I'd come someday. Maybe we've lived a past life together. You were a fisherman and I was a selkie."

"Take off your clothes," he said. "I want to remember more."

Nan slowly stood beside him, a smile playing at her lips. She skimmed her jeans down over her hips and kicked off her shoes, then waited for a long moment in just her underwear.

"What did you do when you thought about your selkie?" she asked.

"What most teenage boys do when they think about naked women," he said.

"Is this why you brought me here?"

Riley shook his head. "I didn't remember until just now. I brought you here because it's one of my favorite places."

"I can see why," she murmured, reaching for the hook on her bra. She tossed it aside, then shimmied out of her panties. "Better now?"

He groaned softly. "It's not a fantasy anymore. It's real."

She rubbed her arms and shivered. "And was it warmer in your fantasy?" Her heart beat a little quicker at the look in his eyes, the barely controlled need sending a shiver through her. "What did you imagine?"

Riley sat up, bracing his hands behind him. "You were standing at the water's edge. That's where I found you, staring out at the sea."

Nan turned and walked across the narrow strip of sand to the water. She dipped a toe in, then winced. It wasn't warm enough to swim, so she waited. A moment later, she heard Riley behind her. He wrapped the blanket around her shoulders and his hand smoothed down her belly. She closed her eyes and enjoyed the touch, moaning as he found the spot between her legs.

Though it was his fantasy, Nan couldn't help but get caught up in it. She tried to imagine what he was thinking, what he might have done to the wild creature he caught.

Nan slowly turned to face him. He stared down into her eyes, then kissed her, his tongue delving deep. Riley continued to explore her body with his hands as if he'd never touched her before. His touch was slow and sometimes hesitant, and then suddenly sure and determined.

When he'd had enough of kissing, he took her hand and pulled her down into the sand. She thought he might strip off his own clothes, but this fantasy must not have gone that far. Instead he gently pushed her back onto the blanket and began to trail kisses from her collarbone to her breasts.

Nan's breath caught in her throat as his lips closed over her nipple. Riley sucked gently, teasing until her nipple grew hard. Then he moved to the other and did the same, her fingers tangling in his hair as his lips teased.

When he reached down between her legs, her breath caught in her throat. When he stopped, she opened her eyes and found him staring at her, a wry smile on his lips.

"What?" she whispered.

"This was always where it ended," he said.

"You just stopped?"

He shook his head. "No, I finished. I never got any further than this before I finished."

Nan giggled. "Well, you've gotten much better at things over the years, haven't you?"

"I have. But I'm not sure I want to ruin the old fantasy."

"Then let me help you," Nan said. She reached down to unbutton his jeans and then slipped her hand inside his boxers. He was hard and ready and she freed him to her touch. "Close your eyes," she whispered.

"No," he said. "I can live with this fantasy."

Nan seduced him slowly, each stroke bringing him closer and closer to ecstasy. She was determined to make the memory exactly how he'd felt it back then, new and baffling and intense. She wondered about the first time he was touched by a real woman. It was one of those stories that they'd yet to tell. She wanted to hear it someday. She wanted to hear it now.

Nan's gaze skimmed over his naked chest and moved to his face. He was the most beautiful man she'd ever known, in body, in heart, in soul. His eyes were closed and his features relaxed. And for a moment, she became the selkie in his fantasy.

The longing for this human life, this experience they shared, was acute. She didn't want to go back to the sea, she wanted to live here with him, to make a life away from everything she knew. The rules were certain. She'd have to surrender her life to him, to toss aside the skin of her old life for a different future.

Did she have the courage to do that? Nan had never made a rash decision in her life, at least not until she'd stepped off the plane at the airport. She had to go back to be sure. It was the only way to test her feelings, to see if they were real.

But would she face the same dilemma as the selkie, unable to return to him once she went back home? There was no magic here. They were living real lives with real feelings. She was in control of her own destiny.

His breathing quickened and he arched into her touch. Nan knew he was close. This was all she'd ever wanted, to please him. She could make a life doing just that and be perfectly happy. But would she always long for the life she left behind? Or could she live here, with him, in complete happiness?

As Riley dissolved into intense spasms, she closed her eyes and enjoyed the sensation of his release. She'd been the one to give him his fantasy. He would remember her once she was gone.

9

THE SUN WAS JUST brightening the sky when the alarm went off. Riley reached for it and pressed the button before it could wake Nan. He fought the urge to set it back in place and go back to sleep. If they overslept and missed her flight, then she'd have to stay for another day or two.

She was scheduled to leave at 11:30 a.m. The trip to the airport would take a couple of hours and check-in was ninety minutes before departure, which meant they had to leave at eight. In two hours.

Carey had volunteered to drive her, but Riley had insisted that the only person with her during her last minutes in Ireland would be him. Riley turned over in bed and let his gaze take in her pretty face. They'd been up late, making love into the early morning hours, and Nan had fallen into a deep sleep. He had tossed and turned for the rest of the night, unable to quiet his thoughts.

He'd given her every opportunity to change her mind, to extend her vacation, to admit that she wanted to stay just as much has he wanted her to. But Nan was determined to go back.

So he'd resign himself to being away from her for a few months. He'd scrape together enough money for a ticket to Madison, Wisconsin, and he'd go there and try to convince her to return. And if she didn't want to, then he'd stay with her. It was a simple plan and the only thing keeping him from going mad.

"Nan," he whispered. Riley smoothed his hand over her face. "Baby, wake up."

"Umm." She moaned and then reached out and pressed her fingers to his lips.

"We have to leave for the airport in two hours."

She opened her eyes and stared at him. "It's today," she said.

Riley nodded. "It is."

She wrapped her arms around his waist and hugged him. "Oh, I'm not ready to go."

He wasn't going to ask her again, Riley thought to himself. He didn't want to make their last hours together difficult for either one of them. "We still have a few hours. You packed last night so you just have to shower and get dressed."

"And make love to you," she said.

"Yes," he said. "We can't forget that."

"I never expected this," she said. "Sometimes, I think I'm living in a dream. I'll get home and I won't believe that I met you."

"I'll call you and remind you," he said.

"Yes, you have to call me. I don't even know your

phone number. I've never called Ireland. And we have to email. And we can Skype."

"Skype is when we can see each other over the internet?"

She nodded. "You have to get broadband or wireless to use it."

"Kellan knows all about that stuff. He'll help me get it set up."

Nan smiled. "Good."

"And what time will be you be home?"

"Probably not until really late. My plane gets in after midnight. And then I have a two-hour drive to get home. So maybe about three in the morning. Which would be…"

"Six or seven hours difference. So, I can call you tomorrow morning at about nine my time. And I'll have slept a whole night without you."

"I'm sure you'll manage."

"I'm going to sleep here for the next month," he said. Riley pulled the pillow to his face. "This place smells like you. Like that lotion you put on after you shower."

Nan reached over and grabbed the bottle from the bedside table and handed it to him. "Here. You can keep it. You can rub it all over yourself when you miss me. Or put it on your pillow before you go to sleep."

"You're not taking any of this seriously, are you?" Riley said.

"No. If I do, I'll start crying and I don't want to start crying." She kissed him. "I will come back. I promised my grandfather that I would. Maybe even for Christmas. That's not that far off. Four months. That will go by so quickly."

"Four months is an eternity."

"How long had it been since you'd slept with a woman before I showed up?" Nan asked.

"Longer than four months."

"So, you know you can do it, right?"

Riley laughed. She obviously didn't understand male physiology. "It doesn't work that way. I was a starving man and you just fed me the most wonderful gourmet meal I've ever tasted. And now, you're going to take away all the treats again and let me starve. And you expect me not to crave them?"

"We'll just have to have internet sex," she said.

"As much as the idea intrigues me, it's not a substitute for you." He paused, then kissed her shoulder. "But we can probably make do."

"Good," she said. Nan sat up, then crawled on top of him, her thighs straddling his hips. Riley stared up at her, realizing this might be the last time they had sex. He had no idea whether they'd be able to survive months apart.

Nan was beautiful and sexy—the kind of woman that any man would be lucky to have. And there'd be hundreds, maybe thousands who were a lot closer to her than he would be by tomorrow.

She smiled down at him as she settled herself against his stiff shaft. Riley reached out and clasped her hips. The temptation to enter her without protection was almost unbearable. But she didn't seem to be concerned. When she leaned forward to kiss him, he probed at her entrance, then waited for her to reach for the box of condoms.

But instead, she simply sank down on top of him. A tiny smile played at her lips and Riley held his breath, wondering if this was all she'd allow. Slowly, Nan began to move, her gaze fixed on his, her eyes glazed with desire.

Though sex with Nan was incredible no matter what the situation, this felt more than extraordinary. Every time she moved, waves of sensation coursed through his body. It took every ounce of his control to keep from coming.

But for Nan, she didn't want to wait. As she increased her pace, he recognized the signs of her pleasure—the tiny furrow on her brow, the way her teeth worried at her lower lip and her quick, shallow gasps with each stroke.

Riley reached between them to touch her and the moment he did, she dissolved into powerful spasms. Bending close, she kissed him and the taste of her mouth was enough to send him over the edge as well.

Though it came quickly, the orgasm was intensely satisfying. It was the perfect end to their time in bed. Riley slipped his hands through her tousled hair and molded her mouth to his. He wanted to say the words out loud. *I love you.* They were there, on the tip of his tongue, the sentiment so real he could feel it deep inside his heart.

But Riley stopped himself. Until she came to understand her own feelings, nothing he said would make a difference. She knew exactly what he wanted and how deeply he felt for her. But at the moment, something or someone was standing in between them.

A soft sigh slipped from her lips and she looked down at him and smiled. "We are good together," Nan said.

"Yes, we are."

She stretched out beside him, her cheek resting against his chest. "I'm just going to lie here until it's time to go."

"You don't want to take a shower?" he asked.

She shook her head. "I don't want to smell like me, I want to smell like you when I get home."

Riley reached out and lifted her lotion from the folds of the quilt, then squirted some into his hand. He rubbed it on his chest and drew in a deep breath. "You're going to have to send me more of this," he said. "I think I'm going to be using it a lot."

Nan laughed, then crawled out of bed. She combed her fingers through her hair and then picked up the clothes she'd left out to wear.

"Give me those," Riley said, holding out his hands.

"You want my clothes?"

He wiggled his fingers and she relented, handing him the dress and her underwear. Riley pulled up the quilt and shoved the clothes underneath.

Nan braced her hands on her hips and shook her head. "What are you doing?"

"I'm hiding your skin," he said. "You're my selkie. Now you can't leave."

"It's not the clothes," she said. "When I set foot in Ireland, I shed my skin. I'm a different person now. I'm your lover and Carey's granddaughter and an Irish citizen, according to you."

He took the clothes out and set them on the bed. "I'm not going to keep you here. But, someday, I hope you'll stay a little longer." Riley drew a ragged breath. "There are so many places we haven't seen yet."

"All right," she said. "Enough. Let's get dressed and we'll have breakfast on the way to the airport."

Riley watched her from the bed, refusing to get up until she was completely ready to leave. With every minute that passed, he saw her slowly leaving him, resigning herself to the fact that their time was over. It was a feeling that made him angry and sad and frustrated all at once. But he wasn't about to ruin their last few hours together.

"I think you need to kiss me again," he said.

She leaned over the bed and brushed her lips over his.

"Just do that every few minutes and I promise, I'll try to be happy."

RILEY PARKED IN the loading zone at the airport, pulling over to the curb before turning off the ignition. Nan had insisted that they say their goodbyes outside the airport rather than dragging it out until the very last second.

She fought the lump of emotion in her throat, leaning against Riley and hugging his arm. "It seems like years since you picked me up. And why did you pick me up in that clown car when you had this car?"

Riley chuckled. "I had new tires put on it in Limerick that morning. That's why I was late. But then, you were late, too."

"I didn't like you very much. I thought you were really full of yourself. But I was wrong."

"And I thought you were the most beautiful thing I'd ever seen."

"You thought I was a flake," she said.

"A very beautiful flake," he said. "But I was wrong, about the flake part."

She took a long, deep breath, trying to control the emotions that threatened to turn her into a sobbing idiot. "All right. So, we're just going to say goodbye and then you'll kiss me and that will be it."

Riley nodded. "Goodbye, Nan."

She smiled, tears filling her eyes. "Goodbye, Riley."

He pulled her into a long, deep kiss, lingering over her mouth until a car behind them beeped their horn. He held her close, his forehead pressed against hers. "Call me as soon as you get home."

"I will."

"I love you, Nan."

Her heart stopped and for a long moment, she couldn't breathe. "I love you, Riley." Knowing that she couldn't take much more, she opened the door and hopped out, pasting a smile on her face. She pulled her bags from the backseat, then stepped onto the sidewalk. Riley got out of the car and joined her, wrapping his arms around her and giving her a fierce hug.

"Go," he murmured, kissing the top of her head. "Before I lock you in my car and take you back home with me."

Nan nodded, then stepped out of his embrace. One last look was all she could manage before she turned toward the entrance. The first step was the most difficult, but Nan put one foot in front of the other and walked through the sliding glass doors.

At the last minute, she looked back and saw him standing outside, watching her leave. He raised his hand to wave and Nan bit back a sob. She gave him a quick wave then strode through the airport.

She was grateful that the Shannon Airport had an office for U.S. Immigration and Customs. The last thing she wanted to do at the end of her trip was wait in line to declare the few things she'd purchased. Nan stood in line and when she reached the agent, she pulled out her passport.

The American woman struggled with her first name. "Tiernan," Nan explained. "Like tears that you cry. Not tires on a car."

"Where do you live?" the agent asked.

"Madison, Wisconsin."

"How long have you been in Ireland?"

"Not long enough," Nan murmured. She glanced up. "Ten days. And nine nights."

"Has anyone asked you to bring anything into the U.S.?"

"No," Nan said.

"Have you received any gifts while you were here in Ireland?"

She held out her hand. "This ring." Nan stared down at the claddagh, the silver heart glinting in the light. She remembered the moment he'd given her the ring, in the fitting room at Burkes. And then again, on top of the wall at the old abbey. The ring had been a pledge, he just hadn't said the words.

"He loves me," Nan murmured.

"What?"

"I don't think I can do this," Nan said.

"Excuse me?"

"I don't want to leave. Can I go back?"

"Why don't you want to board your plane, ma'am?"

"I don't want to leave him," Nan said. "He asked me to stay and I told him I had to go home. But he was right. I don't need to go back. I can stay here with him and be happy."

"Ma'am, your visa is only for three months."

"It—it doesn't make a difference. Can I have my passport back?"

The agent slid it across the counter and Nan grabbed it. "I'm going back," she said, stepping away from the desk.

The agent smiled. "Good luck. And make sure not to overstay your visa."

Nan smiled. "Thanks. But I'm an Irish citizen. I can stay as long as I want." She hurried back to the exit, digging through her purse to find a credit card. She'd have to rent a car, but this time around, she knew how to drive in Ireland. "Bring on the stick shift," she muttered. "I can handle anything."

There was a long line at all of the rental desks and it took nearly fifteen minutes to reach the agent. She put down her credit card. "I need to rent a car," she said. "Something small. A Fiat if you have one."

"Do you have a reservation?" the agent asked.

"No, do I need one?"

"I'm afraid all our cars are booked," the agent said. "Try Enterprise."

Grabbing her luggage, Nan got into another line, but the story wasn't much different. She didn't have a reservation. There might be a car available in an hour or two. If she wanted to upgrade to a luxury car for a ridiculous amount, there was a car available now.

She grabbed a wad of cash from her wallet and headed for the money changer. She had Irish money left, but not enough to get her to Ballykirk. This time, she would convince a cabbie to take her. She put three hundred euros on her credit card and then walked back to the front door.

The cabs were waiting in a long line and she hurried to the first one, leaning into the passenger side to speak to the driver. "How much to take me to Ballykirk?" she asked.

"Is that near Bantry?" he asked.

She nodded. "It's about an hour each way. Two hours round trip."

"Two-fifty," he said.

"I'll give you three hundred," she said.

"Hop in," the driver said.

She felt a tap on her shoulder. "Excuse me, do you have a light?"

Nan froze, the sound of his voice sending a thrill through her body. She slowly turned to find Riley standing behind her. This time, when the tears filled her eyes, she didn't try to stop them. "You're still here," she said.

"I decided to wait until your plane left. Just in case you changed your mind."

"Lass, are you getting in?"

"She has a ride," Riley said.

"With me," the driver said. "She agreed to pay me three hundred."

"Listen, fella, she's my girl. I think I'll be taking her wherever she wants to go."

The cabbie held up his hands. "No problem. I didn't want to drive to Ballykirk anyway."

Nan threw her arms around Riley's neck and hugged him tight. "How did you know I'd come back?"

"I didn't," he said. "I just hoped."

"I was stupid," she said. "I don't want to leave. I don't need to leave. I want to stay with you for the rest of the summer."

"And what about after that?"

"We'll figure that out later," she said.

"No," he said. "If you love me, I want to be with you forever. Not just a few more weeks."

She drew a deep breath. "Then I'll stay forever," Nan said. "This is where I belong."

"Well, then, I think we should go home," he said.

Nan looked up at him and smiled through her tears. "Yes, let's go home."

"The car is in the car park. And don't think I'm going to be carrying your luggage this time around." He grinned, then stepped off the curb to cross the street.

"Maybe I will take that cab," she said.

"All right," he said, grabbing her suitcase and dragging it along behind him. "Don't get your knickers in a twist."

"My knickers are none of your business," Nan said.

"I beg to disagree, Miss Galvin. I happen to be very well acquainted with your knickers. Especially that lovely little thong you like to wear."

"If you're not nicer to me, you're not going to be seeing my knickers for a very long time." He stopped and held out his arm and Nan slipped beneath it. "That's much better."

"Are you hungry, then, or can we just drive home and go right to bed?"

"I could eat," Nan said.

Riley kissed her on the top of her head, pulling her close. "God, I do love you, Nan."

"I know," she said. "And it's a feckin' miracle."

* * * * *

So you think you can write?

It's your turn!

Mills & Boon® and Harlequin® have joined forces in a global search for new authors and now it's time for YOU to vote on the best stories.

It is our biggest contest ever—the prize is to be published by the world's leader in romance fiction.

And the most important judge of what makes a great new story?

YOU—our reader.

Read first chapters and story synopses for all our entries at
www.soyouthinkyoucanwrite.com

**Vote now at
www.soyouthinkyoucanwrite.com!**